DEATH STAR

The bruiser named Barlow held death in his hand. It was called a morning star, a killing tool centuries old, a strand of chain links with two spiked steel balls on one end. Fargo ached to have a gun in his hand to counter it, but his Colt .45 lay far out of reach as Barlow came at him.

Fargo found out fast that Barlow knew how to use the morning star. A flick of his wrist sent the spiked balls sailing downward as they reached the end of the chain. Fargo felt one hit the side of his head as he tried to dodge it, and he cursed with the pain of the blow. He flung himself forward, diving to the ground, but the second of the steel spheres crashed into his shoulder, and he felt the spikes tear through his shirt and flesh.

Agony shooting through his arm, he lay helpless as Barlow got ready to send the spiked balls hurtling at him again. Fargo never thought he'd run into anything that made bullets seem sweet—but this was it. . . .

**BE SURE TO READ THE OTHER
THRILLING NOVELS
IN THE EXCITING TRAILSMAN SERIES!**

SIGNET

TRAILSMAN SERIES BY JON SHARPE

- ☐ THE TRAILSMAN #161: ROGUE RIVER FEUD   (182189—$3.99)
- ☐ THE TRAILSMAN #162: REVENGE AT LOST CREEK   (182197—$3.99)
- ☐ THE TRAILSMAN #163: YUKON MASSACRE   (182200—$3.99)
- ☐ THE TRAILSMAN #164: NEZ PERCE NIGHTMARE   (182219—$3.99)
- ☐ THE TRAILSMAN #165: DAKOTA DEATH HOUSE   (182227—$4.50)
- ☐ THE TRAILSMAN #166: COLORADO CARNAGE   (182235—$4.50)
- ☐ THE TRAILSMAN #167: BLACK MESA TREACHERY   (182243—$4.50)
- ☐ THE TRAILSMAN #168: KIOWA COMMAND   (185153—$4.50)
- ☐ THE TRAILSMAN #169: SOCORRO SLAUGHTER   (185234—$4.99)
- ☐ THE TRAILSMAN #170: UTAH TRACKDOWN   (185382—$4.99)
- ☐ THE TRAILSMAN #171: DEAD MAN'S RIVER   (185390—$4.99)
- ☐ THE TRAILSMAN #172: SUTTER'S SECRET   (185404—$4.99)
- ☐ THE TRAILSMAN #173: WASHINGTON WARPATH   (185412—$4.99)
- ☐ THE TRAILSMAN #174: DEATH VALLEY BLOODBATH   (185420—$4.99)
- ☐ THE TRAILSMAN #175: BETRAYAL AT EL DIABLO   (186672—$4.99)
- ☐ THE TRAILSMAN #176: CURSE OF THE GRIZZLY   (186893—$4.99)
- ☐ THE TRAILSMAN #177: COLORADO WOLFPACK   (187598—$4.99)
- ☐ THE TRAILSMAN #178: APACHE ARROWS   (186680—$4.99)
- ☐ THE TRAILSMAN #179: SAGEBRUSH SKELETONS   (186931—$4.99)
- ☐ THE TRAILSMAN #180: THE GREENBACK TRAIL   (187601—$4.99)

Prices slightly higher in Canada.

Buy them at your local bookstore or use this convenient coupon for ordering.

PENGUIN USA
P.O. Box 999 — Dept. #17109
Bergenfield, New Jersey 07621

Please send me the books I have checked above.
I am enclosing $_____ (please add $2.00 to cover postage and handling). Send check or money order (no cash or C.O.D.'s) or charge by Mastercard or VISA (with a $15.00 minimum). Prices and numbers are subject to change without notice.

Card #_____ Exp. Date _____
Signature_____
Name_____
Address_____
City _____ State _____ Zip Code _____

For faster service when ordering by credit card call **1-800-253-6476**

Allow a minimum of 4-6 weeks for delivery. This offer is subject to change without notice.

THE TRAILSMAN
#182

BLOOD CANYON

by
Jon Sharpe

A SIGNET BOOK

SIGNET
Published by the Penguin Group
Penguin Books USA Inc., 375 Hudson Street,
New York, New York 10014, U.S.A.
Penguin Books Ltd, 27 Wrights Lane,
London W8 5TZ, England
Penguin Books Australia Ltd,
Ringwood, Victoria, Australia
Penguin Books Canada Ltd, 10 Alcorn Avenue,
Toronto, Ontario, Canada M4V 3B2
Penguin Books (N.Z.) Ltd, 182–190 Wairau Road,
Auckland 10, New Zealand

Penguin Books Ltd, Registered Offices:
Harmondsworth, Middlesex, England

First published by Signet, an imprint of Dutton Signet,
a division of Penguin Books USA Inc.

First Printing, February, 1997
10 9 8 7 6 5 4 3 2

Copyright © Jon Sharpe, 1997
All rights reserved

The first chapter of this book originally appeared in
Vengeance at Dead Man Rapids,
the one hundred eighty-first volume in this series.

REGISTERED TRADEMARK—MARCA REGISTRADA

Printed in Canada

Without limiting the rights under copyright reserved above, no part of this
publication may be reproduced, stored in or introduced into a retrieval system, or
transmitted, in any form, or by any means (electronic, mechanical, photocopying,
recording, or otherwise), without the prior written permission of both the copyright
owner and the above publisher of this book.

BOOKS ARE AVAILABLE AT QUANTITY DISCOUNTS WHEN USED TO PROMOTE PRODUCTS OR
SERVICES. FOR INFORMATION PLEASE WRITE TO PREMIUM MARKETING DIVISION, PENGUIN
BOOKS USA INC., 375 HUDSON STREET, NEW YORK, NY 10014.

If you purchased this book without a cover you should be aware that this book is
stolen property. It was reported as "unsold and destroyed" to the publisher and
neither the author nor the publisher has received any payment for this "stripped
book."

The Trailsman

Beginnings . . . they bend the tree and they mark the man. Skye Fargo was born when he was eighteen. Terror was his midwife, vengeance his first cry. Killing spawned Skye Fargo, ruthless, cold-blooded murder. Out of the acrid smoke of gunpowder still hanging in the air, he rose, cried out a promise never forgotten.

The Trailsman they began to call him all across the West: searcher, scout, hunter, the man who could see where others only looked, his skills for hire but not his soul, the man who lived each day to the fullest, yet trailed each tomorrow. Skye Fargo, the Trailsman, the seeker who could take the wildness of a land and the wanting of a woman and make them his own.

Montana, 1860. The early Mexican explorers named it the land of the mountains. The American pioneers knew it as the land cradled by the towering Rocky Mountains, and there were some who wanted to make the evils of another time and another place come alive again...

1

It would have been just another stagecoach to the ordinary observer as it rolled across the Montana territory. But the big man astride the magnificent Ovaro was not the ordinary observer. Some knew him as Skye Fargo. Others knew him simply as the Trailsman, the man who combined experience, instinct, and a special awareness to see where others only looked, to detect what ordinary men missed seeing. His lake-blue eyes were narrowed as he watched the stage move along the road. "Something's not right," he muttered to himself. "I don't like it." He moved the horse forward, out of the trees where the sun made the Ovaro's jet-black fore- and hindquarters glisten in contrast to its gleaming white midsection.

He hadn't had any luck so far, he reminded himself grimly as he thought about the reason that had brought him into the northwest Montana territory. Perhaps things were about to change, he hoped. But his eyes went to the line of rocky hills that ran along the far side of the road. The half-dozen riders disappeared behind a line of tall rocks, but not before he caught a glimpse of them. They had been riding almost all afternoon in the high hills, almost paralleling the stage and holding a steady pace as they moved through the high rocks. It was impossible to tell whether they were watching the stage or just passing the same way, but Fargo decided to stop the stagecoach, regardless, and spurred the Ovaro forward. He quickly caught up to the stage and saw it was no mud wagon with a light-framed top and roll-down canvas windows, but a full Concord coach with a straight-grained white ash frame, side panels of poplar, and running gear of strong white oak.

The lone driver turned in the driver's box to look at Fargo as he came alongside, and Fargo saw a leathery face with a black beard and dark eyes under a worn, floppy-brimmed hat. "Rein up, friend," Fargo called, and the man pulled the two teams to a halt.

"Nothing to rob," the driver said.

"Didn't come to do any robbing," Fargo said and drew closer to the stage. He peered inside at the three fabric-covered seats that could hold nine passengers, and his glance swept the floor as well. But he saw no bloodstains, no bullet holes, no marks of trouble, and he returned his eyes to the driver, who stayed sitting quietly. "Thought you might be in trouble," Fargo said. "I've never seen a big Concord traveling this country without passengers." He paused as his eyes swept the roof rack. "No luggage, either, not even a strongbox." He moved the Ovaro forward and lifted the black canvas to look inside the front boot, then did the same with the long slope of the rear boot. "Nothing, anywhere," he grunted. "What would make a company send out a big Concord completely empty?"

"The stage was a special charter," the driver said. "Paid for by six gents, up from Wyoming. They paid enough to cover the trip back empty." Fargo let his face show that he was impressed as he took in the stage again, the body barn-red, the wheels yellow, and the name of the builder in black letters along the bottom of the body,

Abbot, Downing & Co. Concord, New Hampshire. It was a real Concord, unquestionably, and the driver's explanation seemed reasonable. But not satisfying, Fargo grunted. He'd never heard of a stage line that wouldn't try to fill up their coach, even if they'd been paid enough to make a run back empty. Stagecoach owners didn't turn away from making a double profit. He moved the pinto slowly around the big coach and silently cursed as he saw nothing that suggested any explanation other than what the driver had offered. But there was something wrong. He felt it inside himself, with that sixth sense that seldom failed him.

"Who owns the stage?" he asked.

"Mullevy Brothers. They do short-line charters," the driver said.

"Never heard of them," Fargo said.

"They're new," the driver said.

Fargo nodded and backed the Ovaro from the stage. "Glad you weren't in any trouble," he said.

"Glad you weren't a damn road bandit." The driver sniffed, snapped the reins, and drove away. Fargo tossed a quick glance up at the hills. The riders had gone their way, or they were behind tall rocks, and Fargo moved the pinto slowly along the road. He let the coach roll out of sight as he followed along the road and saw the sun going down over the tops of the Little Belt Mountains. Another hour would bring night, he guessed, and made a wager with himself that the stage wouldn't be driving by dark. He kept the pinto almost at a walk as he followed along the road, scanning the high rocks occasionally without glimpsing the six riders. But they could well be unseen amid the jagged rock formations, he knew, and soon the blue-gray of dusk rolled down from the mountains. Dissatisfaction continued to ride with him. There was some-

11

thing more to the empty stage, he told himself again, though he had to wonder if he were just desperate for a lead that wouldn't prove empty.

He hadn't found himself riding this lonely road for pleasure, he reminded himself, though Paula Hodges still remained a goal, and that would spell pleasure. He pushed aside thoughts of Paula and increased the Ovaro's pace as dusk slid into darkness. He'd gone another half hour when flickering lights broke the stygian blackness of the night, and he finally found himself riding up to three flat-roofed buildings. He reined up in front of the largest of the buildings, where a weathered sign, TRAVELER'S WAY STATION, hung from the top edge of the roof. He scanned the scene and failed to see the stagecoach. His eyes moved along a hitching post, expecting to find six horses, but he saw only two, both already unsaddled. Dismounting, he left the Ovaro at the hitching post and walked around to the rear of the building, where a thin smile touched his face as he saw the big Concord there, horses unhitched, undoubtedly in the nearby barn.

He walked back to the main building and went inside to find a big, log-paneled room with three long dining tables and heavy wooden chairs. A woman in a blouse and skirt, middle-aged with a worn face, cleared dishes from one of the long tables and glanced up at him. A small man came forward, olive-skinned with black hair in need of cutting, small eyes, and quickly offered the edgy obsequiousness of the small-time innkeeper. "Welcome, my friend," he said, and Fargo was surprised to hear a Mexican accent. "A good meal, a good bed, or both?" he added.

"Both," Fargo said. "With a shot of bourbon."

The man spread his hands apologetically. "No bourbon, my friend, but I have good rye whiskey, Old Overholt."

"That'll do," Fargo said, and the man gestured to the woman.

"I am Santo. Welcome to my little inn," the man said, turned to the wall behind him, lifted a large key from a rack, and handed it to Fargo. "Room three. Down the hall."

"Not too busy tonight," Fargo commented. "I saw only two horses outside."

"We are never too busy." The man shrugged.

"I saw six riders earlier—thought they might be headed this way," Fargo remarked as the man poured a shot glass of rye.

"They have not stopped here," Santo said with an air of resigned acceptance.

"I'll bring my saddle in," Fargo said and hurried to the Ovaro, to return in minutes, carrying the saddle. He went to room three and found it small, spare, but clean, made up of a single bed, a battered dresser, a water basin, and a lamp. When he finished freshening up, he went outside to find the woman serving a plate of corned antelope and potatoes that was surprisingly tasty. He had just finished the meal when the stage driver came into the room to ask for a pitcher of water, paused to see Fargo with surprise flooding his face, then apprehension. "This one of your regular stops?" Fargo asked cheerfully.

"No," the driver said curtly and hurried from the room with his pitcher. Fargo downed the last of the rye, and the woman cleared away the dishes, and the innkeeper disappeared into the back of the inn with her. Silence and two candles were Fargo's companions as he waited a little longer before going outside into the warm night. He strolled to the rear of the inn, where he examined the stagecoach in the light of a half-moon, paying special attention to the front and rear boots. But he found nothing and returned to the little room in the building, where he undressed and stretched out on the bed as a warm breeze came through the single window. Eyes closed, the sight of the big Concord rolling empty across the rich Montana territory floated through his thoughts. Anyone else would have paid it no heed, he knew, a big Concord rolling its way. But his sixth sense continued to prod at him. That and the frustration that had become a larger companion each day, and he let the events that had brought him to the Montana territory unfold again in his thoughts.

Roy Averson had communicated with him through Dave Landers only a few days after he'd found a new cattle trail for Dave all the way up from the Colorado territory into lower Montana. The meeting had taken place in a small town just north of Yellowstone, where Averson had waited inside an empty shed with only a table and two chairs as furniture. Roy Averson turned out to be a big man with salt-and-pepper hair, a strong face with bushy, black eyebrows, and the piercing eyes of an eagle. He had a commanding presence, almost lordly, with a deep voice and broad gestures, as though he more properly belonged in another century. The impression was immediately heightened by three objects lying on a piece of burlap on the table, which Fargo quickly recognized from pictures he had seen. Averson was quick to see the moment mirrored in Fargo's eyes. "You know something about medieval weaponry, Fargo?" he asked.

"Not a lot," Fargo said.

"We'll have time to talk about that at a later date. Now we'll concentrate on why I asked to see you," Roy Averson said and drew a thick stack of bills from his pocket and thumped the money down on the table. "That's all yours, Fargo. Dave Landers said you're the very best, and that's what I need, and I'm willing to pay for the very best."

Fargo's quick glance at the stack of bills told him there had to be at least two thousand dollars there. "What do you expect for that kind of money?" he questioned.

"I'm expecting you to find my granddaughter and bring her back to me," Averson said. "They grabbed her with two of my hands when they all went to pick up a Welsh Cob I bought her. My fault. I should never have let her go to get the damn pony."

"Any ideas who?"

"Kidnappers, that's who. I'm expecting a ransom note any day," Roy Averson thundered. "They had to lay low with her for a spell, hide out someplace, because they knew I'd have my men scouring the whole damn countryside for them."

"I take it you did that," Fargo said.

"And found nothing. That's when I came looking for you. They'll be moving her. They can't sit around here, where I'll find them sooner or later. This is the best chance to find her before they hide her away someplace. The child' life is at stake. God knows what could happen to her on purpose or accidentally."

"But you haven't a ransom note yet," Fargo said.

"That'll come. That's just a formality. They know I'll pay anything to get the child," Roy Averson said.

"How old is she?" Fargo asked.

"Ten. She's small and blond, and her name is Amy," Averson said. "From what I hear, if there's a trail to be picked up or a blade of grass out of place, you'll find it, and that's what I want you to do. Find something that'll lead you to her."

"You have any leads?" Fargo asked.

"A few. I'll give them to you. The important thing is that I'm sure she hasn't been moved yet. I've had almost a roadblock around the entire area."

Fargo let a wry sound escape his lips. "You'd need a hell of a lot more men than you have to seal off the whole region," he said.

Roy Averson's mouth tightened. "You're right, of course," the man grunted and put one hand on the stack of bills. "This is yours. I'll give you as much to use to buy information. Cold cash goes a long way to loosen tongues."

Fargo let his lips purse in thought. He had written Paula Hodges he'd come visiting soon as he finished the job for Dave Landers and was there in Montana territory. It was a promise he very much wanted to keep. Paula would be full of waiting passion, and she was too good an old friend and too rewarding a lover to disappoint. Yet he had a little cushion of time before he was expected, and Averson was offering the kind of money only a fool would turn down. Yet there was more, he admitted with an inner wince. He hated to put passion on hold for anything. It was against his principles. But a little girl's life was possibly at stake, and that took precedence over money, passion, or whatever. He let a along sigh escape him as he turned to Roy Averson.

"Where do I communicate with you if I find her?" Fargo asked and saw the man's commanding face take on more satisfaction than gratitude.

"My own property is way up northwest Montana, a place called Blood Canyon. But I figure they'll be moving through this area, and I want to stay close. I've set up quarters in a town called Cutter's Bend at the inn there," Averson said.

"I know the place," Fargo nodded.

"Get word to me there, I hope with Amy," Roy Averson said.

"Let's hear what leads you have," Fargo said, and Averson quickly told him what few leads he had gathered. They had little substance, Fargo noted inwardly.

"I'll be waiting at Cutter's Bend, Fargo. I know you won't disappoint me," Averson said.

Fargo remembered how the man's words proved to be more wishful thinking than realistic as, in the days that followed, he pursued each of the leads, only to find them dissipate into nothing. He thought back to the last one, which had seemed the most promising, a saloon in a miserable little town of a handful of rotting buildings. Someone had seen a man stop there and leave a little girl tied in the saddle of a horse tethered outside. When he visited the saloon, Fargo recalled, he had announced to everyone within earshot his willingness to pay hard cash to find the girl. There had been the usual murmur that disclaimed any knowledge until a short man sidled up to where Fargo leaned against the bar.

"I might know where there's a kid," he said. "I could find out."

"That'd be good," Fargo said carefully.

"How will I know if she's the right one?" the man asked, craftiness in his face.

"I'll go with you," Fargo replied.

"No way. I tell you if she's the right one, you give me my money, and I'm gone. I don't wait around for you to change your mind," the man said. "She got a name?"

Fargo took in the man's shifty-eyed face. Everything about him was run-down, from his frayed shirt collar to his worn clothes. Yet he fit. The information Fargo

wanted wouldn't be coming from upstanding citizens.
"Her name's Amy," Fargo said. "She's small and blond."

"How much?" the man insisted.

"A thousand," Fargo said, deciding to make it something the man would be happy to get. "If she's the right one."

"I'll be back," the man said.

"When?" Fargo asked sharply.

"This time tomorrow," the man said.

"I'll be here," Fargo said. "You've a name, mister?"

"Willie Smith," the man said, and Fargo watched him hurry from the saloon. His eyes scanned the others at the bar.

"Anybody else see the little girl left outside?" he asked.

"I did," a gray-bearded man said, and Fargo grunted. At least Willie Smith hadn't been the only one to see the child. There had been a little girl held on a horse, and Fargo allowed himself a glimmer of hope. This lead was showing more substance than any of the others, and he finished his drink and left the saloon. He bedded down in a clump of ash and was waiting back in the saloon the next day when Willie Smith appeared.

The man hurried to him, licking his lips nervously. "She's the kid you want," he said.

"Where is she?" Fargo questioned sharply.

"Not so fast. My money first. You could get her and not pay up," Willie Smith said.

"And you could have the wrong kid or be making up the whole thing," Fargo said. "Who's got her?"

"Don't know exactly, but they're keeping her in a shack," the man said. "I know where the shack is."

"How many are there?" Fargo pressed.

Willie Smith licked his lips again, and his hands twitched nervously. "They're keeping her alone."

"No guards?" Fargo frowned.

"They don't want to call attention to her," Smith said.

Fargo cursed inwardly. He wanted to reject Willie Smith's answer. It was entirely too convenient. Yet it was just plausible enough to be true. "I still won't buy a pig in a poke," he said. "Take me to the shack. If it's the right kid, you'll get your money. That's as far as I'll go," Fargo said.

Willie Smith spit on the floor, a gesture of anger and unhappy realization. "Let's go," he muttered, and Fargo followed him from the saloon. He rode a few paces behind Willie Smith as the man rode north and down into a small dip in the land. After another fifteen minutes of riding, Fargo saw the shack, standing alone, no horses tied outside, no figures standing guard. "She's inside," Willie Smith said as he came to a halt. Fargo drew up and swung to the ground, then drew the Colt as he approached the shack. Willie Smith dismounted and hurried after him. A lone window let Fargo peer within, where a candle gave enough light for him to see the inside of a shack. A little girl sat on a hard-backed chair, ankles and wrists bound, her hair falling just below her ears on both sides of her face. There was nothing else in the shack except bits and pieces of broken boxes and general litter. The child wore a shapeless one-piece dress that covered her knees.

"I'll take my money," Willie Smith said as Fargo moved to the door of the shack.

"You'll wait," Fargo grunted, opened the door, and stepped inside the shack. The little girl rose from the chair at once. "Easy, honey. No one's going to hurt you," Fargo said as he walked toward the child. She seemed the right age, Fargo observed, her face smudged with dirt, her eyes wide, frightened. He halted beside her, his eyes moving across her hair, a bright, fresh yellow. "What's your name, sweetie?" he asked.

"Amy," the child said, and he peered at the dirt smudges on her face again, then lowered his gaze to her bare arms where there were more smudges of dirt. He brushed his fingers across her left arm. The streaks of dirt didn't come away. They had been there long enough to harden, and he noticed more dirt smudges on her legs. His eyes went to the child's hair again, and he touched the bright yellow shine of it. His lips formed a grim smile.

"You want to give me the money, now?" Willie Smith said truculently, and then his eyes widened as he saw the Colt in Fargo's hand.

"How about I shoot your kneecap off, instead?" Fargo asked.

"What's wrong with you?" Willie Smith frowned.

"I don't like to be taken," Fargo said, saw the small pitcher of water beside the chair, and picked it up. With a quick motion he poured it over the little girl's hair. The child gave a tiny shudder as the water hit her, but she didn't move, and Fargo watched as it took only moments before part of her blond hair developed streaks of brown. "Amateur job," Fargo bit out. "Probably peroxide with nothing else to hold it."

He turned to Willie Smith, his eyes blue ice. "How'd you know?" Willie Smith asked.

"You should have cleaned her up all over," Fargo said. "You take her off some nearby farm?" The man's truculent silence was an answer. "You saw a chance to make some money and jumped at it," Fargo went on. "You did a quick job on her hair to produce a kid to fit the one I'm looking for. Did you really think you could pull it off?" Again, silence was his answer as Willie Smith shifted his feet uncomfortably. "Take her home and get out of my sight before I lose my temper," Fargo rasped and strode from the shack.

It had ended there, another lead that, despite its early promise, had frittered into nothing, and Fargo turned the thought off in his mind as he lay on the bed. Since the last lead had unraveled, the frustration had grown stronger, and he realized that when he spotted the stagecoach he was alert for anything that caught his eye. The empty stage still jabbed at him as he lay on the bed. Somehow, somewhere, there was something wrong, he told himself again before he drew sleep around himself and let the night go its silent way.

He woke with the morning and allowed himself the luxury of the bed for a little while longer before he swung to his feet and used the washbasin. He heard the sounds of the stage horses being hitched as he dressed and decided to leave his saddle in the room as he went down for breakfast. He walked along the hallway of the inn when he heard Santo talking, then the voice of the stage driver. "That is for the extra dinner and the extra bottle of water, senor," Santo said.

"All right, here," the driver grunted, and Fargo heard the sounds of the coins being spilled onto the table. He stayed back against the wall of the corridor and heard the driver hurry from the inn. Moments later, he heard the big Concord pulling away from the inn, and he stepped from the corridor into the main room. The woman brought him a mug of strong coffee, which he downed with long sips as Santo returned.

"Good morning, senor," the innkeeper said cheerfully.

"I heard the stage driver pay you for an extra dinner,"

Fargo said. "Why would a man order two dinners and extra water?"

The innkeeper shrugged. "Maybe he was very hungry and very thirsty," the man said.

"And maybe he wasn't alone," Fargo thought aloud.

"I see nobody with him," the innkeeper said with another shrug.

"Couldn't he have brought somebody in the rear door without your seeing him? The stage was right against the door," Fargo said.

Santo frowned in thought. "I suppose so. I am up front mostly," he conceded.

"And he could have brought someone down before you woke up this morning," Fargo said.

"I guess so, senor," Santo agreed.

Fargo took a handful of coins and put them on the table as he finished his coffee and strode back to the room to get his saddle. It was time for another look at that empty Concord, he muttered inwardly. It was time to see whether his sixth sense had been as acute as it usually was.

2

It was only minutes later that Fargo sent the Ovaro streaking from the way station at a full gallop. It wasn't long before he came in sight of the big Concord, still rolling empty along the road, and he snapped a glance at the hills. His gaze swept the tall rocks, seeking a glimpse of the six riders, but he saw only a flight of golden plovers, and he hurried after the stagecoach. When he drew alongside the Concord, the driver half turned to frown down at him. "You again?" the man snapped.

"Rein up," Fargo said sharply, and the driver drew the two teams to a halt.

"What now? You're getting to be a pain in the ass, mister," the man said.

"That's been said before," Fargo said and nodded. "Get down and stand away from the coach."

"What's with you, mister?" The driver frowned, but obeyed. He wore a Remington-Beals, five-shot, single-action piece with a hand-operated cylinder, Fargo saw—no shooter's pistol, yet weapon enough to kill at a fair range.

"Why don't you put your hands on your head?" Fargo said.

"C'mon, this is a crock of shit," the driver protested.

"Indulge me," Fargo said pleasantly, but the man saw

his eyes were icy blue agate and put his hands atop his hat. Fargo nodded in satisfaction. It would add awkwardness, extra motion, and extra seconds in reaching for his gun. Moving along the red side of the stage, Fargo peered into the interior again, felt along the sides, and carefully examined the rear boot. He went forward and peered into the front boot, assuring himself it was empty. Taking hold of the iron rail, he pulled himself up onto the driver's box, the square seat bordered by black iron rails on both sides, large enough to hold a driver and a shotgun rider side by side with their legs dangling down to the front boot.

Fargo sat down on the seat, rose, turned, and peered down on the wood top of the seat, then felt the frown gather on his brow. "It's high," he muttered aloud. "Higher than any I've ever seen." He made a fist with his right hand and pounded the seat. "It's hollow, too," he said when sudden movement caught the corner of his eye. He half whirled, one knee atop the driver's seat, and saw the driver on the ground, reaching for his gun. Fargo's hand shot to the big Colt at his side, and the gun leaped into his hand as the stage driver fired from a half crouch. The driver's bullet passed to his left as Fargo fired a single shot, and the driver doubled over as he fell to the ground to lay motionless, his gun falling from his fingers.

Fargo had already turned, his fingers pulling at the edges of the seat. He felt it lift, pulled harder, and the wooden seat came up in his hands to let him stare down into the space that had been built under the seat. A small figure lay there on her side, knees drawn up so she'd fit, a kerchief over her mouth, her wrists bound. He removed the kerchief and lifted her from the space, and blond hair fell against his face as he propped her up in a sitting position. "It's all right, you're safe now," Fargo said as the child stared at him with wide blue eyes searching his face. He undid her bonds and decided events had moved too fast to take anything for granted. "What's your name, honey?" he asked.

"Amy," she answered in a quiet but firm voice.

"Who's your grandpa? What's his name?" Fargo pressed.

"Grandpa Roy," the child said, and Fargo felt a surge of relief go through him. It was a short-lived feeling as the sound of galloping horses erupted, and he gazed across the roof of the stage to see the six riders racing toward him from the distant rock formations. He leaped from the stage, reached up, and pulled Amy down with him. They'd not be aiming at her, but stray bullets could kill as thoroughly as accurate ones.

"Get under the coach," he said as he pushed her beneath the thoroughbraces and against the left rear wheel. Moving away, he crouched behind the rear boot and raised the Colt as the riders neared. He waited, let them get off their first round of shots that plowed into the body of the coach, then fired, and two of the men toppled from their horses. But he was already following another as the first two hit the ground, took aim and fired, and the rider jiggled in his saddle before he fell. Amy lay flat, pressed against the wheel of the coach, he noted as the other three attackers came around the two teams to approach the stage from the other side.

The nearest attacker bent low in the saddle to get a better angle for firing under the coach. He never got the shot off, nor did he ever get to straighten up as Fargo's bullet caught him in the breastbone. He stayed low over his horse until he finally pitched forward to be kicked in the head by flying hooves as he fell. The last two attackers pulled their horses in a tight circle as they turned to flee, and Fargo drew a bead on one, fired, and saw the man clutch at his shoulder as he raced away. Fargo rose, ran forward, and glimpsed the two attackers racing away on the other side of the coach, the attack at an end. He reloaded, holstered the Colt, and brought the child out from beneath the coach. "It's over, Amy," he said and held one arm around the child. She stayed quietly at his side, no trembling to her, he noted, her small face serious but composed. She was plainly a very contained little girl, he decided. "I'll drive the coach and you can sit inside. It'll be more comfortable for you that way," he said. Amy nodded, unsmiling, and dutifully went into the big Concord, where she all but disappeared inside the wide body.

Fargo climbed up onto the driver's box, put the seat back in place, and snapped the reins over the horses. The teams moved the coach forward at once, and Fargo saw the Ovaro trot along at the rear of the stage as they rolled on. He allowed a feeling of satisfaction to sweep through him. His suspicions had been right. The empty stage had been more than it seemed to be. Amy's kidnappers had decided it would be the perfect cover to transport her, an empty Concord just rolling along. And as insurance, they'd sent the six riders to watch over it from a distance.

But their best laid plans had gone astray, and Fargo enjoyed the feeling of triumph. He drove the teams at an even pace, stayed to the winding roads that took him north past Grizzly Peak, and finally across the Yellowstone River near Big Timber. It was a good way to Cutter's Bend, and he stopped twice to look in at Amy. "By the way, I'm Fargo," he introduced himself at one point. "It was your grandpa who hired me to find you."

"I guessed that might be so," Amy said with unsmiling seriousness and settled back inside the coach. When evening approached, he found a clear pond and stopped alongside a stand of tanbark oak. Amy stepped from the Concord and drank thirstily at the pond, politely accepted a strip of dried beef jerky from him, and maintained her contained composure. She was a most unusual ten-year-old, he decided, seemingly mature beyond her years, yet very much the little girl in every outward appearance. He decided to probe gently with her as she sat beside him.

"Did the men who took you tell you why they did?" he asked.

"No," Amy said softly.

"They mention any names?"

"No."

"You hear them say where they were going to take you?" Fargo asked.

"No. They didn't talk where I could hear," Amy said.

"And you couldn't see anything from where they held you inside the coach," Fargo said.

"Nothing," Amy said and returned to her composed silence. She slept curled up almost in a knot some dozen feet from him as the night grew deep and stayed that way until morning broke. She washed at the edge of the pond, and her contained composure stayed with her as Fargo resumed the journey. He skirted towns, held to the roads that varied from rough to almost impassable, and it was late afternoon when he reached Cutter's Bend. He drove the coach up to the inn, where he saw three men outside. Two of them rushed inside as Fargo rolled the coach to a halt, swung from the driver's box, and opened the coach door for Amy. Seconds later, Roy Averson rushed from the inn and caught Amy as she ran into his arms. "By God, by God," he chortled as he swung the child in a circle and Amy squealed with delight. Fargo followed as he strode into the inn and sat Amy atop a table.

"What about the pony, Grandpa?" the child asked.

"We have the pony, sweetheart," Roy Averson said.

Fargo watched the satisfied little smile pass across Amy's face, and he found himself peering at the little girl. She'd asked nothing about what had taken place, no mention of how she'd been rescued, no rush of gratitude, no explosion of childish anxieties, only the one, cool, single-minded question. It would have been surprising in anyone, much less a ten-year-old, Fargo reflected.

"You rest in the next room. We'll be on our way soon. I want a word with Fargo first," Averson said to Amy, and the child walked into the adjoining room with cool unhurried aplomb. Averson turned to Fargo. "A remarkable little girl," he said.

"She sure is. Most kids I know would be an emotional wreck by now," Fargo said.

"Yes, but now as for you, Fargo, I want to give you a bonus. I never expected results this quickly. How'd you do it?" Roy Averson asked.

"They were clever but they forgot the little things. Always a mistake," Fargo said.

"Only if you meet a man who sees the little things," Averson said and Fargo allowed a half shrug. His glance at the table saw that Averson had brought along the three medieval weapons.

"Fascinating, aren't they?" Roy Averson said. "They're the latest in my collection. I have them shipped from Europe to me. They're not only intriguing, but, except for firearms, they're still more effective than any weapons we have today." He picked up one of the weapons, a steel shaft with a length of serrated chain links at one end that were attached to a heavy steel ball from which five vicious spikes protruded. "You know what this is, Fargo?"

"Yes. It's called a morning-star. I've always felt it was a poetic name for such a vicious weapon," Fargo said.

"Indeed. How do you come to know of it?" Averson asked.

"A traveling salesman stopped in a village where I was for a week. He had a book on the Middle Ages with pictures of knights and weapons," Fargo explained.

Averson hefted the weapon and let the spiked ball make a small rotation. "It'll beat any tomahawk or knife or saber. I've had a smithy make a dozen for my people," he said as he put the weapon down.

"You really admire those days," Fargo commented.

"Not only for their weaponry. They had a lot going for them in governing, in the relationships between people. In some ways they had a much better system than we have today," Averson said. "Come visit me at my place, and we can have a longer talk. Get yourself to Blood Canyon and ask around. You'll find me. Meanwhile, here's your bonus. You did a fine job," the man said and peeled another three hundred dollars from his roll of bills.

"I was taught it was bad manners to turn down a man's generosity. Much obliged," Fargo said. "You going to take care of the Concord?"

"I'll arrange to have it sold," Averson said and called into the other room. "Amy, Mister Fargo's leaving. Thought you'd like to say good-bye to him," he said.

Amy came from the room at once. "Thank you for rescuing me. I hated being cooped up inside that coach," Amy said with more matter-of-factness than gratitude, Fargo felt. Again, he was amazed that there was no sign of being distraught from her ordeal. It was as though she were more mildly annoyed than upset.

"Glad I found you, Amy," Fargo said. "I'm sure you've

lots of reasons to be happy at being back with your grandpa."

"Yes, he's very good to me," Amy said, still without any change in her composed little face, and Fargo frowned inwardly at her self-concerned choice of reasons.

"You'll come visit, I hope," Averson said as Fargo nodded good-bye and turned to leave. Outside, he led the Ovaro away in the gathering dusk as he reflected that Amy was a most unusual child. For some reason he was bothered, he realized. He felt more like a man who needed a drink than a man who ought to be happy at a job well done. He passed a stable that advertised outdoor pens and a hose supplied for grooming your own horse and guided the pinto into the nearest of the pens.

The prospect of grooming the Ovaro held a cathartic appeal, and he paid the stable boy who came forward and proceeded to give the horse a thorough hosing. He used the dandy brush next, then the stable rubber, and finally the hoof pick. When he finished, the horse glistened as the last of the dusk turned to dark, and he felt less unsettled, though he still wondered why the coolly contained composure of a child should have bothered him as it had. But then things that didn't fit right always bothered him. That was, ironically, what had brought his attention to the coach, he reflected. He led the Ovaro into the streets of the town and tethered the horse outside the saloon. Inside, a young woman in a short, satiny dress and eyes too old for the rest of her, showed him to one of a dozen round tables on the sawdust floor. She quickly made certain that he understood he could have drink, food, or other pleasures. "Good bourbon and a good meal," he said, saving the prospect of other pleasures for Paula Hodges.

When he finished the leisurely meal, he went outside

to where the Ovaro gleamed in the light of a three-quarter moon. Two figures stepped from the shadows, and he caught the glint of gunmetal in their hands as they flanked him. "Don't move or you're a dead man," one said as they stepped closer. Fargo eyed the taller of the two.

"Let me guess. You're the two that got away," Fargo said.

"My shoulder's hurtin' fierce, damn you," the man behind him said, and Fargo felt the Colt pulled from its holster. "Get on your horse, and don't do anything stupid. I'd like blowing your damn head off."

Fargo pulled himself onto the Ovaro as the two men swung onto their horses, flanking him on both sides with their six-guns trained on him. "How'd you find me?" Fargo asked.

"We saw Averson, figured you'd be connecting up with him sooner or later," the taller one said.

"Now what?" Fargo asked as he rode between the men down the dark street.

"You're going to help us get the kid back," the one with the injured shoulder snapped.

"How?" Fargo queried.

"We haven't figured that out yet. We want to get you out of town first," the other one said. Fargo stayed silent as the two men steered him out of town and toward a stand of hackberry. When they reached the edge of the trees, he cast a glance at the man with the wounded shoulder and saw the pain in his face. He'd be first, Fargo told himself. He had the Colt, and he'd not moved quickly.

"Who are you working for?" Fargo asked from under the trees.

"What makes you think we're not on our own?" the taller one answered.

31

"Because you don't have the smarts to have figured out moving the kid by the Concord," Fargo said.

"Shut up," the wounded one snarled, and Fargo heard the pain in his voice. "Let's stop a while. This shoulder's killin' me," he said to the taller one, who reined to a halt.

"On the ground," the man ordered Fargo, who nodded and leaned to his right as if he were beginning to swing from the saddle. The wounded one was beside him, but Fargo let his body block the view for an instant as he reached down and drew the thin-bladed throwing knife from its calf holster. The blade in his hand, he half turned as he seemed about to swing to the ground and flung the knife with a quick, upward motion out of the palm of his hand. The man saw the blade as it was almost on him. He tried to twist away, but the pain in his shoulder slowed his reaction time by precious split seconds. The stiletto-thin knife hurtled into the side of his neck, and his mouth fell open with a last gasp. But Fargo was already diving at the man, slamming into him and sending him sideways off his horse.

Landing atop the man as he hit the ground and the horse bolted, Fargo grabbed the Colt out of the man's belt as two shots rang out. Both hit the virtually lifeless figure as Fargo rolled across the ground, came up hard against a piece of log, and felt the crack against his head. He saw pinwheels of brightly colored lights explode in front of him, but he fired off three shots as he shook his head to clear it. Dimly, he heard the sound of hoofbeats racing away as he rolled again, lay still, and let the pinwheels of light subside. The trees took shape again, and the pain in his head was a sharp reminder that the unexpected had nearly ended his best laid plans. He rose, retrieved the double-edged throwing knife, cleaned it on the grass, and returned it to its calf holster. The remaining man was gone, racing for his life, Fargo knew as he holstered the Colt. He'd not come back, not alone, Fargo was certain. But who was he racing away to tell?

The thought hung in his mind as Fargo found a spot deep in the hackberry to bed down. Roy Averson had said Amy had been kidnapped for ransom, a crime committed strictly for money. Maybe that was so, but Fargo grimaced. He had a strange feeling about the kidnapping, one he couldn't define. Yet it persisted. Perhaps his sixth sense working again, he grunted as he pushed aside thoughts and plunged into sleep to wake only when the morning sun flooded the woods. After washing at a pond, he headed west along the edge of the Yellowstone, turned north, and rode through long fields of alpine sunflowers, blue columbine, and wild geranium. The richness of the Montana territory showed itself as he saw herds of white-tailed deer, antelope, and bighorn sheep. Grizzly rose to watch him in all their towering majesty, and he glimpsed a mountain lion prowling across a high ridge. Beaver, martin, and badger were all over, as was the black-footed ferret when he traveled across open land.

He found the valley Paula had written him about when the peaks of the Big Belt Mountains rose up directly in front of him. Heading into the valley, he finally saw the sprawling town of Three Springs, which formed the hub of a web of hog, poultry, and goat farms. Memories flooded over Fargo at once. When he'd first known Paula back in Kansas, her folks had raised poultry. Besides helping with the poultry farm, Paula had assisted the town's only doctor in everything from keeping appointments to emergency operations. Paula was also one of the kindest people he'd ever known, someone who really cared for others, always ready to help anyone who needed help.

Then one day he'd never forget, a band of half-drunken bushwhackers hit town, and Fargo's jaw tightened as memories grew stark. They took offense at what someone said, but that was only an excuse for them to shoot up the town. Paula's folks were gunned down in the wild shooting spree as they ran from town. Fargo recalled again how he had tracked bushwhackers down and ended their short and ugly careers. He'd become very close with Paula after that, and they had stayed close until she decided that home held too many painful memories. She sold the house and went westward into the new frontier lands of the Montana territory. She'd settled in with her base stock to supply the new towns and settlers with the eggs and poultry they'd need.

She'd written often about her new life, and her old yearnings for him, and had described the farm so well it seemed a familiar place when he rode up. As he dismounted, the barn door flew open, and Paula came running out, her ample breasts bounding with beautiful wildness as they always had, and then she was tight against him, sobbing and laughing at the same time. "Let me look at you," he said, stepping back as he took in the round face that hadn't added a line. Paula had always had an open, soft pleasantness to her, round cheeks and full lips and big dark eyes with brown hair cut short. She had always carried a few extra pounds and still did, he saw, and she still wore them well. The added fleshiness was part of what gave her an incongruousness that was uniquely hers, that of an earthy Kewpie doll. "Same as ever," Fargo said as she led him into the house, where he quickly saw a sturdy structure of three rooms with solid furniture and quilted rugs.

"You picked the right day to arrive," Paula said. "I've

had a rabbit stew cooking in the pot, with potatoes, onions, and chives."

"Sounds wonderful," Fargo said.

"Bring your things in while I finish up outside," Paula said, and he brought in saddle pack and saddle, then turned the Ovaro loose to graze. His eyes swept the chicken houses and the yards and he saw that Paula had a good mixture of Barred Plymouth Rock and White Leghorn.

The last of the day slid away, and soon he was sitting across from her, enjoying the hearty meal as they talked of yesterdays. Before the moon was high, he was in the bedroom, watching Paula shed clothes, round, smooth shoulders appearing first, then the full, deep breasts, each a creamy pillow tipped by a prominent dark red nipple on an equally large red areola, breasts made for smothering and enveloping. Just below, a wide rib cage followed, and below that, the round, fleshy belly, a convex invitation of itself that curved down to a dense, jet-black nap that capped the smoldering earthy aspect of her. Thighs were as he remembered, a little heavy, but soft and smooth as those of a girl fifteen years younger.

He watched her brown eyes deepen as he pulled off his clothes, and she took in the smoothly muscled contours of his body. Her hands came out pressed against his chest, slid downward as, with a deep groan, she came forward to press her breasts into his face. Fargo let his mouth open, took in each, pulling gently, then harder, caressing their creamy softness, moving from one to the other and back again as Paula moaned softly. "Yes, oh, my God, yes, yes . . . remembering . . . so good," she murmured as she pressed her breasts into his face. Turning on her back, she let his lips pursue an invisible line around each red nipple, then down across her rib cage, and pause to nibble on the convex mound of her belly.

"Ah, ah . . . ah, yes, yes," Paula cried out as his hand found the dense black nap, pushed through its wiry softness to the very soft Venus mound below, then sliding lower, touched the edges of the eternal portal and found it already moist and waiting. Paula's full-fleshed thighs fell open at once as a low, throaty sound came from her, and he explored further. "Yes, oh migod, yes, yes, like always, like before . . . before . . . please," Paula breathed, running words into one another as her thighs lifted and stayed poised until he brought his torso over hers, pressed down against her, his hot, throbbing erectness against the dense, black nap. Paula half screamed and her thighs closed around his hips, tightened, loosened, tightened again, and her pelvis rose upward, half twisted, one way then the other, the lock seeking the key.

"Oh . . . oh migod, oh yes," Paula moaned as he slid forward into the dark, soft wetness, feeling her close around him, embrace unlike any other, and memory again flooded over him as Paula began to move—long, slow thrustings in which her entire body moved, breasts rising to come against him, hips pushing into him, her full-fleshed thighs sliding along his legs. Every part of her joined in her passion, her entire being immersing itself in pleasure. It had always been that way with her, and it was so now again, wonderful remembrances coming alive, yesterday's ecstasy finding itself again. He thrust with her, joined with her wonderful rhythm and slowly escalating pleasure until Paula was a moaning, twisting, thrusting vessel of ecstasy and the moment finally refused to be held back. She clung to him as though she could turn herself inside him, and her cries echoed in the night as her pubic mound slammed against him again and again and again.

"Oh . . . oooooh, God," she groaned finally, still wrapped around him, and he held her until she finally let her arms and legs go limp and fall away from their grip on him. He lay half over her, still with her, and saw her round-cheeked face wreathed in the afterglow of pleasure, her deep breasts and full-fleshed body still throbbing. Definitely an earthy Kewpie doll, Fargo thought and smiled as he lay quietly with her. "It was worth all the waiting, Fargo," Paula murmured, drawing his face down to the pillowy breasts.

"For me, too," he agreed, and she gave a satisfied little sound as her eyes closed and she stayed in his embrace. The night passed softly, and he woke with her as a new day came.

"How long can you stay?" Paula asked, her first words after she woke.

"I'm in no hurry to go after last night," he said and smiled.

"Last night was only a beginning," Paula said, her eyes dancing, and she purposely brushed both pillowy breasts across his face as she rose. Her promise was kept, and the days became mere interruptions between the nights. They plunged themselves into the lazy totality of pure pleasure, and in between making love, talked of everything from yesterdays and moments never forgotten to questions about her safety today. He felt for Paula, as he always had. She was a thoroughly nice person besides her other qualities. One afternoon as he finished feeding chores with her, he paused to let his gaze sweep the high land beyond the valley. This was Nez Perce and Flathead land with some Northern Shoshoni and Bannock, none of them with the fierceness of the plains tribes, yet none welcoming to the white man.

"They leave us pretty much alone," Paula said, reading his thoughts as he scanned the land.

"Why?" he asked.

"Don't know exactly. I think maybe because here in the valley most everyone's a small farmer or raising hogs, sheep, and fowl, such as I do. No one goes into Indian land hunting their game, the buffalo, antelope, deer, mountain goat. I think they don't see us as a threat," Paula said.

"My experience tells me the Indian sees every settler as a threat," Fargo said.

"We also have a tight warning system. Everyone takes part in regular patrols and lookouts. We're a tight little group. I feel safe here," she said.

"Hope so," Fargo said, putting aside concerns, and the days and nights continued to blend together in an unbroken tapestry of pleasure. It was the fifth or sixth morning—he'd lost count of days—when Paula woke early.

"Stay there. I've two bushels of eggs to deliver to Sam Macavoy. I'll be back in an hour," she said.

"I'll have breakfast ready," he said as Paula dressed and hurried from the house. He allowed himself another half hour of laziness before he rose, washed, and pulled on Levi's. He was at the stove, his back to the door, when he heard a sound and thought it was Paula already returning. He turned to look and saw the three men, each with a six-gun in hand, facing him from the doorway.

"Don't do anything stupid, mister," one growled, young-faced with small eyes. "Come outside." Fargo eyed his Colt in the holster hanging over the bedpost in the next room and decided there was no way he could reach it in time. The men stepped back to let him go through the doorway and outside. He found himself facing a young woman clothed in riding britches and a white shirt. Thick dark-blond hair fell around a strong but beautiful face with a thin, straight nose, good cheekbones, lips perhaps a little thin. But it was her eyes that held him, almost opaque, a blue that was nearly colorless, yet they burned with a pale fire. She was fairly tall, with a straight, commanding posture, narrow-hipped and lean, yet her breasts gave the shirt definite contours. He saw the pale blue-fire eyes flick over the muscled smoothness of his torso before they returned to his face.

She took a step forward, her hand suddenly coming up to slap him across the face. "That's for taking Amy," she hissed. He was still blinking in surprise when she slapped him again. "That's for not minding your own goddamn business," she said. Fargo's hand shot out, closed around the front of her shirt, and started to pull her to him when he felt the muzzle of the revolver pressing into his midsection. He uncurled his fingers and released his hold on her shirt.

"You're living dangerously, honey," Fargo growled.

"Not nearly as dangerously as you," the woman returned, keeping the gun on him, a big Remington single-action piece with a brass trigger guard.

"Who the hell are you, and what's Amy to you?" Fargo spit out.

"They were bringing her to me until you stuck your nose into it," the woman said.

"You snatched her from Roy Averson?" Fargo frowned.

"A mother's got a right to take her own kid back, doesn't she?" the young woman snapped, and Fargo felt himself staring at her as the frown dug deeper into his brow.

3

"You telling me you're Amy's mother?" Fargo asked, the frown digging deeper into his brow.

"The one and only," the young woman snapped.

"Why'd you have to kidnap her?" Fargo questioned.

"To get her away from Roy Averson," the woman answered.

"He's not her grandfather?" Fargo asked.

"Oh, he's her grandpa, unfortunately."

"And your father."

"That's how it works," the young woman said with grim sarcasm.

"This isn't making any damn sense to me," Fargo said. "You stole your own daughter from your own father."

"Bull's-eye," the woman said, and Fargo saw her almost opaque blue eyes peering hard at him, probing, plainly wondering. "I thought the Concord would be a perfect cover for moving her. You must be very good. What do they call you?" she asked.

"Skye Fargo. Some call me the Trailsman. What do they call you?" Fargo asked.

"Dulcy Washburn," the young woman said.

"Where's Mister Washburn?"

"Dead, years ago."

"Why'd you have to kidnap Amy?" Fargo questioned.

"To get her back. He took her from me, six months ago," Dulcy Washburn said.

Fargo's eyes narrowed on her. "I'd say there's no love lost between you two," he commented.

"That's putting the best face on it," Dulcy shot back, and Fargo continued to regard her. In her tall, unbending, icy demeanor he could see Roy Averson's commanding presence. Like father, like daughter, he wondered.

"What's the worst face?" he asked.

"Hate," she said, biting out the word.

"How'd you find me?" Fargo queried.

"Been searching for that Ovaro of yours. You don't find many like that," she said.

"You didn't come just to tell me you're mad about my taking Amy," Fargo said.

"You're right there. You took her. You're going to get her back for me," Dulcy Washburn said.

Fargo let a wry snort escape him. "Forget it, honey. I was paid to do a job, and I did it. I didn't know anything else then, and I'm not interested in anything else now. Go take her back yourself."

"I can't get to her. You can," Dulcy Washburn said. "You'll get her back."

"No, thanks. This is a family feud. I'm too busy enjoying myself," Fargo answered.

"You'll do it if you want to see Paula again," Dulcy said, and Fargo took a step toward her, then halted as he saw the Remington still in her hand.

"You've got Paula?" he asked.

"She's safe. It depends on you if she stays that way."

Fargo found himself spearing Dulcy Washburn with fury and astonishment in his eyes. "You little bitch," he hissed.

"Thank you," she said with wry sarcasm. "I want Amy

back. I want her out of that monster's hands. I'll stop at nothing to do that. It's your call, Fargo. Amy for your little bedmate Paula."

Fargo let thoughts race through his mind. There were too many things unclear, too many elements that needed explaining. But one thing was clear. Dulcy Washburn meant every word she'd said, and that made Paula a pawn who could end up an innocent victim caught in a whirl of events far beyond her. He needed to buy time for Paula, and that meant knowing a lot more than he did. "I go along only if I know everything about this. Straight talk or no deal," he said.

"That's fine with me," Dulcy said.

"And I don't work under a six-gun," he added.

She didn't pause to think, but dropped the Remington into its holster. "Fair enough," she said and turned to the three men. "Wait by the fence," she ordered, and Fargo followed as she went into the house where her almost opaque eyes lingered on his smoothly powerful torso. "You want to dress?" she asked.

"Not yet. You bothered?" Fargo said.

Dulcy allowed him a wry smile. "No, but you're a lot handsomer than I expected. I appreciate beauty, in horses, dogs, or men," she said. Her smile broke the commanding severity of her face and gave it a different flash of beauty. "Ask your questions, Fargo," she said.

"First one is what's this all about. Seems to me you're making a pawn of a ten-year-old, your own child," Fargo said, accusation in his voice.

"I'm taking her away from a bad influence. Roy Averson's my father, but he's a no-good, rotten bastard. He's a crazy, unprincipled, ruthless man," Dulcy Washburn said.

"I got the feeling Amy liked him," Fargo said.

"Of course. He gives her everything she wants to keep her happy. She's very important to him, for the wrong reason," Dulcy said.

"What would that be?"

"Amy's worth a lot of money. She had an aunt, Clara Averson, who left her a fortune, which she'll get when she's sixteen. Meanwhile, whoever's acting as her guardian gets three thousand dollars a month."

"That's real money," Fargo murmured, his brows lifting.

"If she's with him, he gets it, and he wants that money," Dulcy said.

Fargo shot her a narrow glance. "If she's with you, you get it. Seems to me you both have the same reason for wanting Amy," he said.

"Only I'm her mother. She's supposed to be with me, and I've her best interests at heart. Keeping her out of Roy Averson's hands is the first part of that. He's an evil man, I tell you. You've no idea how evil, but you'll find out," Dulcy said. "He lied to you about Amy being taken for ransom. He knew I was behind it. He just didn't know how I'd get her back to my place. That's what he needed you for."

"Yes, he lied to me on that," Fargo admitted.

"And you're wondering if I'm lying to you about him," Dulcy said.

"The thought crossed my mind," Fargo conceded.

"I'm not going to try to convince you I'm telling you the truth. It'd be just words and you want more than that," Dulcy said, and he nodded. "Get Amy. That's first. The rest will follow," she said.

Fargo let his lips purse as the thought prodded him. It was worth a try. "Give me a reason to believe in you. Let Paula go now," he said.

"And you can just walk away from getting Amy," she said.

"I won't. You've my word on that. I don't give my word 'less I mean to keep it," he said.

She thought for a moment. "Even the best of us can change our minds. Too many things can happen to do that. No, Amy first. I learned to play poker a long time ago. I'd be a bad poker player if I gave up my ace in the hole. Amy, then the girl goes free." Her pale, blue-fire eyes didn't flinch, her face a beautiful sculpture made of ice.

"You say your pa's a ruthless man. I'm thinking you're both cut out of the same cloth," Fargo said.

She stepped forward and put the palms of both hands on his chest, then held them there, a warm, sensuous touch. "You're wrong. I'll prove that to you. That's my promise," she said.

"But Amy comes first," he said.

"That's right."

He snorted, but realized he was forming an grudging admiration for her hard-nosed, unswerving determination. "You know where I find Blood Canyon?" he asked.

"Due north."

"Where do I find you?" Fargo asked.

"Not far from Blood Canyon. West, the DW ranch," Dulcy said.

"How many hands do you have?" Fargo queried.

She allowed a wry smile. "Enough, but not as many as I used to have, thanks to you," Dulcy said.

"That's your fault," Fargo said.

"I'll be waiting for you," she said and took her hands from his chest, but not before she let them slide down to his waist. She seemed a combination of opposites, ice and fire, he decided, and watched her walk from the house, back straight, steps firm, yet her flat rear moved with a definitely sensual swing. Did the flesh reflect the spirit, he wondered. He turned away and finished dressing, saddled the Ovaro, and rode into the midmorning sun. He didn't consider trying to see if Paula was being held at Dulcy's place. Dulcy would know better than that, and he rode north, the mountain peaks to his left.

He set a steady pace, and by the day's end he rode carefully, the signs of Indian all around him. He bedded down under a big rocky mountain maple and listened to the howl of timber wolves until he finally slept. When morning came, he rode along a stretch of open land bordered by hackberry, and as the day went on the land grew wilder. Yet he saw clusters of houses, small settlements, and found fast-running, wide streams where placer miners seemed to be a fixture. He halted beside one miner at a wide stream, and the man paused in sifting water through his wash pan. "Blood Canyon," he said.

"Another four miles along the stream," the man said, and Fargo rode on, followed the curve of the wide stream, and saw the canyon come into sight. He was surprised to see that it seemed more a deep, wide valley than a canyon. He was also surprised to see a number of houses and small ranches that seemed to ring the canyon but with plenty of land between them. Passing a neatly tended ranch, he saw two young girls working in a corn field and a man plowing more land behind them. He passed more ranches and saw the figures of men and women on the land, everyone bent on some chore or another. He was nearing the north end of the canyon when he reined to a sudden halt and astonishment flooded his face.

It seemed as if he were suddenly in another country and another century. Suddenly, it was as though he were in an English countryside in the Middle Ages. Rising up in front of him was a castle built of great stone blocks, replete with high, round corner towers, an outer bailey lined with embrasures, a gatehouse, drawbridge, and a moat fashioned from a nearby stream. In the center of the castle, an inner bailey or keep rose up behind the outer fortifications, the entire structure a smaller version of the great medieval castles.

Fargo stared at it, hardly able to believe his eyes, yet it was there, rising up, refusing to be disbelieved, a castle in the middle of the Montana territory, in the shadow of the Rocky Mountains. He moved the pinto forward and saw three men on guard in front of the drawbridge, looking somehow out of place in their cowhand's clothes and carrying rifles. He walked the horse across the drawbridge, and one of the guards halted him. "Roy Averson. Tell him Skye Fargo's come calling," he said, and one of the men hurried through the tall gate and into the interior of the castle. He returned in moments and waved Fargo forward. Keeping the horse at a walk, Fargo rode into the big inner court and saw more men near the walls, tending to their horses, others working at hay troughs, still others doing stonework. In the distance, at the other end of the big, open court, he saw Amy working with the sturdy Welsh Cob pony.

Roy Averson strode from inside the castle, and Fargo dismounted. "Well, good to see you, Fargo," the man said. "You're surprised, of course. Most people are."

"Make that one more," Fargo said.

"See to Fargo's horse," Averson said to one of the men who quickly came to lead the Ovaro away. "We've a fine stable at the rear of the outer bailey," the man said as he led the way into the keep or center of the castle.

"I'm glad I had the chance to read that traveling man's book on the Middle Ages. I'd be completely at sea without it," Fargo said as he found himself inside a big dining hall with a long wooden table and a collection of medieval weapons against two of the walls. He saw the dozen or so morning stars, the same number of battle axes, and two flails, the long, straight lengths of spiked steel attached to a chain and pole. All were ugly, deadly weapons, and alongside them stood over a dozen long poles, each some fourteen feet tall, each tipped by a different blade. They were called polearms or pikes, each designed for a special attack. The gisarme could slash and stab a man at the same time, the glaive, partisan, and halberd each fashioned to inflict their own brand of wound. He even had three catchpoles, Fargo noted, huge two-pronged blades of fishhooklike attachments that could grip a rider and drag him from his horse.

"My collection is an indulgence, but they have already proven how effective they are. When we first started building, there were Indian attacks. These medieval weapons made short work of the Indians. They don't come into the canyon now. They're afraid of the castle," Roy Averson said and sat down at the long table. He clapped his hands, and a stooped man in a white apron appeared with a tray that held a wine bottle and glasses. "Join me, Fargo," Averson said as he filled the glasses. The wine, Fargo found, was a delicious, full-bodied red, and Fargo let his eyes go over the vast interior of the castle."

"It must have cost a pretty penny to build this place," he remarked.

"Indeed. I hired a full crew of stonemasons, imported craftsmen, and paid them well," Averson said. "But the castle and the weapons are not mere indulgences. I've taken my interest in the Middle Ages a lot further than just that. I've combined the best of then and the best of now. My people use rifles as well as flails and pikes. You see, there was a great deal of good in the social relationships of those days. Actually, it was much better for the common man than it is now."

Fargo's brows lifted. "I always heard the common man was pretty much a serf, owned and ruled by his master," he said.

"A broad misconception. Let's look at the lot of the average man today. If he's a small farmer, he exists only if he can sell his products. If he's a hired hand, he's at the mercy of his employer. He sells his services, his labor, to a wealthy landowner. Something goes wrong, they get fired or take sick, they're on their own, adrift. The landowner, their boss, has no obligation to them. They sell their services, and he pays them for it. That's all there is, nothing else. The little man has the freedom to be poor, that's what it comes down to."

"And in the Middle Ages?" Fargo questioned.

"The king or lord demanded labor and sometimes tribute from those who worked for him, but for that he had the obligation to see that all his people were fed, clothed, and protected. There was a real social contract, not just a for-hire arrangement. The common man had all his needs taken care of and was much better off for it."

"Some folks put a high value on being free," Fargo said. "They're willing to take being poor for it."

"Not so many as you think. You saw the small ranchers in the canyon, I'm sure," Averson said, and Fargo nodded. "I've worked out a modern version of the old feudal system with them, and they're grateful for it. They supply me a certain portion of their labor, their earnings, or their production, and I guarantee them their shelter, food, medical care, and protection from Indians, bandits, or any other threat. It's not quite the same as the old feudal system, but it retains all the good parts. My families know they won't be fired or their incomes cut off. They know they're under my protection. They do their part and they're able to live without fear or worry."

Anything further he was going to say was interrupted by Amy as she strode into the castle and gave Fargo a glance that was at best cool politeness. Turning to Averson, she clipped out her words. "Richardson keeps arguing with me about how I'm training the Cob," she said.

"He's an old man. He's set in his ways," Averson said placatingly.

"He's out of line, and he's useless. Let him shovel shit in the stables. That's the best place for him," Amy snapped and stalked away, plainly certain she'd have her way.

Fargo glanced at Roy Averson, who half shrugged apologetically. "She has very definite opinions," Fargo commented.

"Yes. Amy's an unusual child, wise beyond her years," Roy Averson said. "And she's why you've come visiting. Dulcy's been to see you, I'm sure."

"She has, but I came because I don't like being lied to," Fargo said. "Amy wasn't taken for ransom. You knew Dulcy was behind it."

"Would you have taken the job if you knew her mother had her?" Roy Averson asked blandly, and Fargo knew he hadn't an answer. "I suppose she told you her usual pack of lies about me," the man said.

"She didn't have anything good to say about you," Fargo admitted. "She said you took Amy because she means money to you, and that's all you care about."

"Amy means money. I won't deny that, but that's not why I took her. She's here because Dulcy's not fit to raise her. It's hard to say that about your daughter, but Dulcy is a selfish, unprincipled, ruthless bitch. She's an evil young woman," Roy Averson said.

"This has a familiar ring to it," Fargo remarked.

"I'm sure it does. God knows what she's told you about me, but I'll wager she didn't tell you anything about herself. Did she tell you she lived in a whorehouse for two years with Amy, a place owned by a friend of hers?"

"No, she didn't," Fargo admitted.

"A whorehouse. Is that your idea of a place to bring up a little girl for two years?" Roy Averson tossed at him.

"Can't say it is," Fargo said and nodded.

"You ask about her husband?" Averson queried.

"She told me he's dead," Fargo answered.

"But she didn't tell you she killed him, did she?" Averson snorted.

"No, she didn't," Fargo said.

"Dulcy only cares about Dulcy, nobody else, not even her own daughter. She wouldn't care if someday Amy became a fancy girl or ran a whorehouse. She doesn't take the time to teach her anything. All she does is keep the child under her thumb. She wants to break Amy's will."

"From what I've seen of Amy it wouldn't be easy to do that," Fargo said.

"But Dulcy can do it. She wants it so that when Amy reaches sixteen, Dulcy will have her under complete control. That's all Dulcy cares about, controlling everyone and everything, especially Amy and her inheritance. If she's a mother, she's a mother from hell," Roy Averson thundered.

Fargo contemplated everything the man had said. Averson was confirming one thing above all. Perhaps because they were two sides of the same coin, father and daughter hated each other with a vitriolic passion. That fact wouldn't normally be his concern, except insofar as it made his task more difficult, but there were truths he had to find out before he could decide his next moves. Were it not for Paula, he'd ride away from this thorn-filled thicket of lies and counteraccusations, but he didn't have that choice. He had to stay and try to find out as much of the truth before he acted. Roy Averson's voice cut into his thoughts.

"Let me show you around the place a little more," the man said, and Fargo followed as Averson took him on a tour of the inside areas of the castle, the great common rooms, the huge hearth, and the inner chambers. When they went outside, he showed Fargo around the outer parameters as Fargo made mental notes of every detail. Roy Averson showed off his castle with a combination of regal pride and childlike enthusiasm. When he finished, Fargo concluded that for all its imposing grandeur, the castle was but an echo of what the great medieval castles must have been. Yet it was formidable enough, he realized.

"Very impressive," he said as Averson's tour ended at the drawbridge, where he was quickly reminded that the man was not simply a strange, bizarre buffoon immersed in his own fantasies but a very shrewd and sharp adversary.

"I'd guess you've seen everything you came to see, Fargo. I presume you've made a rough guess of the height of the walls and turrets and noted the embrasures as to their number and placing." Averson smiled, and Fargo was silent as he swore inwardly. "I know Dulcy sent you to take Amy back," Averson said and laughed. "I hope you've seen enough to know that you'd die in any attempt."

"It'd take a lot of doing," Fargo agreed.

"How much did she offer you?" Averson asked.

"Nothing," Fargo said. It was not exactly a lie. There had been a demand, not an offer, and he wanted to deny Averson his assumptions. "I told you, I came because I didn't like your lying to me and because I was curious," Fargo added.

Averson's shrug was part concession. "Good enough reasons, I'll admit," he said.

"I might even stop by again. I'd like to try some of those old weapons," Fargo said.

"Anytime," Averson said. He was a thoroughly confident man, Fargo realized, secure in his power and his position. He called for someone to bring Fargo's horse, and Fargo waited as Amy rode into view on the sturdy pony. Amy's eyes lingered on the Ovaro as the horse was brought, and Fargo climbed into the saddle.

"That's a horse I'd like," Amy said.

"A lot of people have said that." Fargo smiled.

"Maybe nobody's offered you enough," Amy said.

"Nobody has enough money," Fargo said. "I met your mother, Amy," he added. "She asked about you."

"That's nice. Tell her I'm fine," Amy said, no inflection in her voice.

"If I see her again," Fargo said blandly.

"You will," Amy said and walked the Cob away.

Fargo heard Roy Averson chuckle. "She knows her mother," the man said.

Fargo let his eyes move out beyond the drawbridge. "How'd this place get the name Blood Canyon?" he asked.

"The tribes used to make the canyon their major battleground. Legend is the canyon ran red with blood. They did the same with any settlers until I came into the canyon. The place is very well named," Averson said, and

Fargo had the distinct feeling that the canyon would continue to live up to its name. He was about to leave when a man came from the interior of the castle, a big, burly figure with powerful neck and shoulder muscles, a heavy face with thick lips, black hair, and almost black eyes. A mouth that turned down added to the picture of excesses and cruelty. "This is Barlow, Fargo, my right-hand man in today's terms. In the Middle Ages he'd be my squire," Averson said.

Fargo nodded at Barlow and saw the man wore two heavy-handled Smith & Wesson rim-fire Army pistols. "Roy told me about you," the man said to Fargo. "Seems you're real sharp-eyed."

"I try to be," Fargo said.

"Sometimes it's good not to see too much," Barlow said evenly.

"Never went along with that," Fargo said.

"What you don't know won't hurt you," Barlow pressed.

"Never went along with that, either," Fargo said and turned to Roy Averson. "Maybe I'll come visit again." He walked the horse across the drawbridge and the moat where three rifle-bearing guards remained an incongruous trio against the castle walls. He rode on and down the center of the canyon, took in the figures working their lands along the periphery of the canyon, and decided not to stop. There were too many questions he had for Dulcy before he could go on, and so he turned the horse west when he reached the end of Blood Canyon.

He found a stand of white fir as dusk turned to dark and brought the horse beneath the wide-branched conifers. He dismounted and had just unsaddled when he caught a faint sound, tight fir cones being brushed against each other. He whirled, dropped into a crouch, the Colt in his hand, and saw the three near-naked figures step forward, bows drawn, arrows in place. Fargo's finger began to tighten on the trigger of the Colt, confident he could take the three braves, when another sound came from behind him. He flung a quick glance over his shoulder to see three more braves with bows drawn and arrows aimed at him. Out of the corner of his eye he glimpsed two more braves. The three had become eight, all with arrows aimed—more than even the quick-firing Colt could outshoot at such close range.

He turned his eyes back to the first three as another figure stepped forward, a short man wearing only a breechclout and an armband. Black hair hung long and unkempt around a young but severe face. "You talk Shoshoni?" the Indian asked.

Fargo considered a moment. He knew some Shoshonean, which the Bannock, Ute, and Comanche also spoke, but he preferred a tongue he knew better. "Crow," he said, choosing a tongue used by most tribes as a working language.

The man halted a few feet from him, his black eyes narrowed. "You come from place of evil spirits. We watch, always watch. We kill everyone who comes from place of evil spirits," the Indian said, and Fargo saw the Northern Shoshoni designs on his armband.

"You kill everyone you catch alone," Fargo said. The Shoshoni grunted, the sound an admission. "You watch place of evil spirits by sun and by moon?" he asked, leaning heavily on his Crow.

"We watch," the Indian said, and Fargo wondered if Roy Averson knew of the Indian surveillance. If so, he had seized on a perfect way to rid himself of someone who could be a problem without dirtying his hands. Fargo tabled the thought for the moment. It was an academic question for now, made so by eight very real arrows. The Shoshoni motioned for the Colt, and Fargo decided to see how far he could push back.

"I am not of the place of evil spirits," he said and dropped the gun into its holster. The Indian's face darkened, and he slammed his fist into his hand. Fargo made no move, and the Indian raised one arm in a gesture to the surrounding braves. "I am not of the place of evil spirits," Fargo repeated.

"We will see," the Indian said, and Fargo swore silently at the answer. They would see by torture and come to the answer they wanted to come to. He had the unenviable choice of dying now or dying later. He decided on later and the chance to buy some time. Lifting the Colt out of the holster, he handed it to the Shoshoni, who held it in his hand as the other braves came forward. They let Fargo saddle the Ovaro and climb onto the horse before bringing their own ponies, surrounding him, and moving forward. The Shoshoni with his Colt rode in front of him, the others on both sides and behind him, and Fargo saw that they turned northwest and stayed in the firs. His mind raced as he went over what few options he had. They had stayed outside the canyon before jumping him. They rode at an unhurried pace with him. Overconfident, he grunted. But there were too many for him to use the knife in his calf-holster.

He had to move with startling boldness to have any chance, and he let his captors ride another two minutes before he lifted his voice. "I will speak now of the place of evil spirits," he said and reined to a halt. The Shoshoni holding the Colt turned to face him as Fargo held his right palm out and upward. The Indian held the gun almost casually, Fargo noted. A quick glance at the others showed that none had arrows on their bowstrings. He guessed he could seize thirty seconds if exploded fast enough.

"Speak," the Shoshoni said, and Fargo let the Ovaro move a few paces closer, until he was but a few feet from the Indian.

"You let me live afterward," he said and inched another step closer.

"Speak," the Shoshoni said, his face stone. Fargo started to lower his hand when he shot his arm forward with the speed of a lightning strike. His hand closed around the Colt, and he yanked the gun free, turned it in his hand, and fired. The Shoshoni flew backward from his pony as his abdomen exploded in red, and then Fargo, head down, was spraying shots in a half circle as he dug heels into the pinto's ribs. He saw at least three of the Shoshoni go down; another clutched his belly and fell forward on his pony as the Ovaro leaped forward. Staying flattened on the saddle, Fargo had the horse into a gallop, swerving in a tight circle as the shouts of pain, alarm, and confusion came from behind him. The Shoshoni still able to ride started to give chase, but he was already streaking away through the firs. He raced the horse back into the canyon as he glimpsed three Indians giving chase. When he nosed the horse downward into the canyon, he saw them rein to a halt, pause, and finally turn to go back.

He halted beside a big boxelder just inside the slope of the canyon walls, decided it would make a prudent place to bed down, and he swung from the horse. He set out his bedroll, undressed, and stretched out in the warm night. He had let himself grow careless about the Indians. They were always a presence, always posing a danger, and he'd have to keep that in mind. But they were a peripheral danger for him. The real danger lay in finding a way to save Paula, and he thought about Roy Averson and Dulcy. One or the other was lying to him. One or the other was twisting the truth, trying to give themselves the best of it. Or—he felt a frown dig into his brow—they were both telling the truth.

The thought hung in his mind, shimmering with an evil light of its own. Two sides of the same coin, he reflected again. Both ruthless, both unprincipled, both willing to use a child as a pawn for their own ends? He'd said as much to Dulcy, and she'd been quick to deny it. He'd wanted to believe her, but Roy Averson had been detailed in his indictment of Dulcy, while she had flung generalities of evil. Fargo closed his eyes to sleep, aware that right now Paula's life hung on a web of accusations, and he knew he'd need more than that.

4

He rode through the bright morning sun, taking note of the Indian pony tracks as he did, and it was past midday when he was surprised to come onto a small town. A weathered sign at the outskirts proclaimed the name: BIG DUSTY. He was not surprised to see a saloon, but his brows lifted when he came to a bank that called itself the Northwest Savings Company. He paused at a man standing outside. "Looking for the DW spread, Dulcy Washburn's place," he said.

"Stay north out of town. You'll see it," the man said, and Fargo rode on, followed a wide stream, and finally found a corral of posthole fences with some two dozen Herefords inside. He turned down a road toward a low-roofed, sturdy house fashioned of logs and quarry stone. Dulcy emerged from the house as he rode to a halt and dismounted, and he took in her full figure clad in Levi's and a yellow shirt. She managed to appear practically efficient and very feminine at the same time, he noted.

"You're alone, I see," she said, the pale blue-fire eyes more opaque than usual.

"You figured that," Fargo shot back. "You knew I wouldn't come back with Amy. You just wanted me to see his damn castle."

Her shrug was a concession, and he followed her into

the house, where he found himself in a spacious living room with a large sofa, quilted rugs, and solid furniture, a comfortable, warm room. "I wanted you to see for yourself what it'll take to get Amy," she said.

"It'll take a hell of a lot," Fargo growled.

"That's why I'm hoping you can talk your way into getting her," Dulcy said.

"I doubt that, especially after what he said about you," Fargo answered.

She gave a small smile. "He gave you his usual assortment of half-truths, of course," she said.

"Was that what they were?" Fargo pushed at her.

"Exactly. I expect he told you about Sam Washburn," Dulcy said.

"He said you killed him. It's hard to make a half-truth out of that," Fargo said.

"But he didn't tell you why. He didn't tell you I shot him to stop him from beating Amy and me. It was his habit. He'd get drunk and go crazy. I was his main target. He did it once too often," Dulcy finished. The explanation was one he could appreciate, but he heard no hint of remorse in her voice. But then perhaps that was too much to expect, he decided.

"What about living in a whorehouse with Amy for two years?" Fargo questioned.

"We were hiding out," Dulcy said, and Fargo frowned back. "From Sam's brother. From Roy, too. Sam's brother came looking for us, especially me. When he finally got himself killed in Kansas, I left the whorehouse with Amy. Till then, it was the best place to hide out. My friend didn't ask anything of me except housekeeping," Dulcy said.

Fargo thought about her words. Explanations given in matter-of-fact tones, no excuses and no apologies, all reasonable enough with nothing to make him disbelieve her.

Yet they were still only words, her own contradictions to Roy's accusations, and he had already learned that Dulcy had more than enough steel inside her. Her voice cut into his thoughts. "What else did he tell you?" he asked.

"He gave me a tour of the castle, and he told me about his philosophy about how things were better for the little man in the Middle Ages," Fargo said.

"And how he's the protector of all the farmers and ranches in the canyon?" she asked with sudden harshness.

"Yes, he did," Fargo said.

Dulcy let a sharp laugh escape her lips. "Jesus, that's a good one," she snorted.

"Before we go on, how did your pa come into this preoccupation with the Middle Ages?" Fargo questioned.

"Aunt Clara lived in Europe. He worked for her there for fifteen years. I lived there in her home, and she sent me to the best schools in Europe, mostly in France and Switzerland. Roy Averson fell in love with the idea of being a lord in the Middle Ages. It stayed with him, and he brought it back here," Dulcy said.

"He said he'd modeled an arrangement with the farmers and ranchers in the valley based on the social contracts of the Middle Ages. He said it was better for the small farmer than anything we have today," Fargo recounted.

Dulcy gave a harsh laugh again. "Better for him. No medieval serfs were ever more completely owned by their masters. He's their lord, and they're his serfs. He controls them, owns them, runs every part of their lives with his men and that bastard Barlow."

"His squire, Roy called him."

"Squire, tax collector, hatchet man, now or in the old

days, it's the same thing. He's the lord's enforcer," Dulcy said.

"How'd your pa manage to own all those people, in your words?" Fargo asked.

"By sucking them in. By lending them money, talking them into borrowing to buy livestock and equipment until they were so in debt to him that he owned them, their very lives, everything they are and everything they have. Little by little he's getting title to their lands, too."

"Why? Doesn't seem to me he wants to become a rancher."

"He doesn't, but the land up here is rich with precious ores, not only gold and silver, but platinum, emeralds, and rubies. I've even heard of diamond deposits. That's why there's a bank in Big Dusty. People from the north and up in Idaho need a bank for their transactions, deposits, receipts, and transfers to other big banks back east."

"I wondered about that bank," Fargo said.

"All the payments from Aunt Clara's trust for Amy come through the Northwest Savings Company," Dulcy said. "Roy Averson wants the land for what it might be worth. He can't mine it and find out until he has it, but that won't take much longer. Those poor fools are as trapped as any serf ever was."

"I've trouble believing that," Fargo said.

"Believe it. He even claims the droit de seigneur," Dulcy said.

"What's that?"

"It means the right of the lord. In the Middle Ages the lord had the right to be the first one to screw the bride, anyone's bride, or any woman he wanted. It was part of his privilege, his right as the lord. All he had to do was invoke the right before the wedding night. Roy Averson's broadened it to take in any girl reaching sixteen."

"You serious?" Fargo frowned. "He gets away with this?"

"For the same reasons the medieval lords did. He's their master. He holds them in his hand, by debt, by force. He has them terrorized physically, bankrupt financially, and drained morally. When people are owned, they're owned, whether it's by a real lord of the Middle Ages or a make-believe one today. A serf's a serf, whether it's because he has no right to own anything as in medieval times, or everything's been taken away from him. That's what all his bullshit about protection and social contracts really means. You can't believe it? Go talk to Harry Crew, Jed Offerman, and Ben Bentley. They're the first places you see when you go into the canyon. Find out for yourself. I tell you he's an evil man."

"Dammit, I think I'll do just that. I want to hear from somebody besides you and Roy Averson," Fargo said.

"Ask about Loretta Crew. She's just turned sixteen. I know she's in line for a visit from the lord," Dulcy sniffed disdainfully.

The frown stayed on Fargo's face as he strode from the house with Dulcy behind him. "I'll be waiting," she said with a smugness he found irritating. He swung onto the Ovaro, put the horse into a trot, and rode back the way he had come. He skirted the town, and the day was beginning to wind to an end when he rode into the canyon. He pulled up at the first ranch, corrals filled with sheep where two men were talking over a fencepost. As Fargo rode up, a woman came from the house, middle-aged, graying hair pulled back, and wearing a black dress.

"Harry Crew?" Fargo asked, and one of the men, a tall,

thin figure and a lined face with pain in his crinkled blue eyes, turned to him.

"I'm Harry Crew," he said. "This is my wife, Emma, and our neighbor, Jed Offerman."

"Dulcy Washburn asked me to come have a talk with you. My name's Fargo—Skye Fargo."

"Sorry, Fargo, you tell Dulcy nothing's changed. We won't help her. She knows why," Harry Crew said. "She's got no right sending someone to do her asking."

"Help her what?" Fargo questioned as he swung from the horse.

"Standing up to her pa. She's wanted us to help her do that all along, and she knows we can't," the man said.

"She really asked me to come see you about helping yourselves," Fargo said agreeably.

"She always says that, but it's really about helping her. She asks things of us we can't do," Harry Crew said.

"Maybe you can do them," Fargo said.

"No, there's no way. Everybody knows that," Harry Crew said and glanced at Jed Offerman.

"He's right," Offerman agreed. "You've got to understand the situation. If Roy Averson calls in what we owe him, he could turn us all out. We've roofs over our heads, we can work our lands, try to pay off our debts, and we're under his protection. We're grateful to him for that."

"I understand you all pay a damn high price for that," Fargo said.

"There's nothing we can do about that, none of us," Harry Crew said. "Not until we pay off what we owe."

The door of the house opened, and a girl came out, long brown hair, liquid, dark eyes, a sweetly pretty face. She wore a loose gray dress that all but hid an understated figure. "Loretta?" Fargo asked, and the girl nodded. "Dulcy Washburn mentioned you," he added. Loretta

Crew returned a surprisingly mature smile that held an edge of sadness in it.

"I know why," she murmured.

Fargo peered at her. "That all you can say?" he queried.

"Yes," she said softly.

He glanced at Harry Crew. "You, too?" he asked, and the man looked away, his face tight. Fargo scrambled through his mind for the right words when six horsemen appeared, riding hard to rein up at the ranch. He saw Barlow at the head of the group, the man's beetling, black eyebrows lowering to peer at him.

"Didn't expect to find you here, Fargo," Barlow said.

"Thought I'd pay a visit," Fargo said.

"Can't see a reason for you to do that," Barlow said, displeasure in his hard stare.

"I like visiting," Fargo said blandly.

"I don't know if Mister Averson's going to like that," Barlow said.

"Tell him I'll pay him a visit tomorrow. I don't want him to feel slighted," Fargo said.

"You'd best do that, Fargo," Barlow said and turned to Harry Crew. "Mister Averson will be wanting her tomorrow night," he said with a nod to Loretta. "I'll be by to get her. Have her ready." Barlow didn't wait for an answer, but rode away with his men following, and Fargo turned to Harry Crew, Offerman, and Emma Crew. As he stared at them, he realized he wanted to summon understanding and found he could only feel rage. Contempt erased compassion. Incredulity got in the way of sympathy.

Yet he knew he was wrong to condemn, to be carried away with anger and a sense of towering injustice. His will had not been stripped from him; his spirit had not been crushed. It would take more than words to help these people, he realized. They needed a massive transfusion of hope, some way to renew spirit and will, some way to restore dignity and courage. Yet as he stared at them, he knew the overwhelming meaning of frustration. The task seemed beyond reach. But he swore inwardly. He had to make an effort, find a way. He had at least to try.

"You can't let him do this," he said to Harry and Emma Crew. "You can't let him exercise his goddamn privilege. Stand up to him for Loretta. Fight back. Say no, dammit."

But it was Loretta's voice that answered. "I don't want that. Willie Wrightson tried that. They killed him and took Betsy away. I don't want my parents killed," she said, stepped forward, and put a hand on his arm, her deep, liquid eyes reaching into him. "But thank you for trying. I know you want to help and that means a lot, even if we can't take you up on it. Your wanting to help makes me feel better. We borrow strength from others, even strangers, though I don't feel you're a stranger. I feel you're a friend."

He stared at her sweet loveliness, so young, yet really so much more mature than her elders. "I'm not finished," he said. "I won't let him do this, not to you."

"You can't stop it. Loretta told you what happened to Willie Wrightson," Jed Offerman cut in. "We don't want to sound ungrateful, but we know what's happened before. We know our limits."

"Maybe you don't. I'll be back tomorrow," Fargo said and saw Loretta's deep, liquid eyes follow him as he swung onto the Ovaro. He rode away with rage seething inside him. It was still with him when night came and he reached Dulcy's place, where the door hung open, a kind of mocking invitation that was echoed in her eyes as he strode in.

"Was I wrong?" she asked, sitting back on the sofa, her breasts pushing out her yellow shirt as she leaned back almost insouciantly.

"No," Fargo admitted. "But they see you as having your own axe to grind."

"I know."

"Maybe I can get to them in my own way," he ventured.

"You believe now what I told you about Daddy dear?" she asked. "You still think we're both cut out of the same cloth?"

"Maybe not exactly," Fargo said, willing to make that much of a concession.

She smiled, a hint of triumph in it, and she rose and drew him up with her. "Stay. I've a cooked ham and vegetables on the fire. What are you drinking?" she asked.

"Bourbon," he said and walked beside her into a large kitchen, where a heavy table took up one corner. She produced a bottle of good Kentucky bourbon, and he savored the taste of it as she set dinner on pewter plates. "You were right," he told her as they ate. "The people in the canyon are beaten, broken inside. They've nothing left inside themselves. They need someone to help them."

"They share in whatever they are now," Dulcy said, and Fargo peered at her and saw the icy beauty that held her face.

"You saying it's not Roy Averson's doing? That's sure a change of heart," Fargo commented.

"No change of heart. Of course it's his doing. I told you he's an evil, ruthless man. But they listened to him because they wanted too much too quickly. They helped him put them where they are. I can't have sympathy for their greed and their weakness," Dulcy said, and the pale, blue-fire eyes searched his face. "You think I'm being uncaring?"

"Maybe," he said.

"I just don't want you to get sentimental over them. I'm not uncaring. They don't deserve your sympathy," Dulcy said, and her hand came out to cover his. "You're special, I know. You care about others. That's a wonderful thing, but it should be kept for those who deserve it."

"Such as you." Fargo smiled.

"Such as Amy," Dulcy said, her even-featured face unsmiling. "And I think you need some proof that I'm not uncaring." She rose and stood before him. He watched as her fingers undid the buttons on her blouse. "More than words," she said as she finished undoing the blouse, drew it from her, and he stared at wide shoulders, a little bony, pronounced collarbones, and breasts that seemed to suddenly blossom into round fullness, smoothly tanned, nipples standing erect and dark red on lighter red circles. They seemed larger and fuller than they actually were against the leanness of her torso, and she made a flicking motion with her hand and her skirt and half-slip fell to the floor.

His eyes moved over a flat abdomen, an almost concave little belly with a vertical indention in its center. Trim, narrow hips only slightly flared from a narrow waist and a deep, almost incongruously thick, intensely black V beckoned at the juncture of legs that retained shapeliness despite being thin with long, muscular calves. He rose as she moved and led him out of the kitchen and into a bedroom, where a lamp burned on low and lighted a room painted pink with a wide bed covered with a deep red comforter. He undid his gunbelt and let it slide from his hips, and her fingers were working furiously, helping him shed clothes. The unvarnished wanting of her seemed an invisible net that enveloped him, and he felt himself growing, rising, hardening, captive of a sensuous spell she wove with purposeful abandon.

"Oh, yes, yes," Dulcy breathed as he sank down on the bed with her, and his mouth closed around one full breast, found its firm softness, and his lips pulled on the small, erect tip. Her hands dug into the back of his neck, and he felt her neck arch backward. "Jesus, yes, oh, God, yes ... good, oh good, good," she whispered and moved the breast inside his lips, pushed it upward so her nipple touched the roof of his mouth. She writhed, twisted, and her lean legs came up, rubbing up and down against his sides as urgent, groaning noises came from her. She pressed her body hard against his, then moved her torso back and forth against him, sliding upward and downward, yet kept her breast in his mouth. "Mmmmm ... mmmm ... yes, yes ... oh, yes," Dulcy moaned, and suddenly her arms were around him, and she tore her breast from his lips to clap her legs around him, open them, and clap them hard against him again.

"I want, I want," she murmured, a steely demand in her throaty cry, and he felt the tremendous power of her wanting. Arms, legs, breasts, mouth, everything enveloping him, rubbing, pressing, crushing against him with a frenzy that commanded and demanded, sweeping all subtlety before it. He felt her back arch as his hand slid down across the almost concave belly and pushed into the very thick nap, rubbed onto the soft-hard pubic mound, and caressed the protrusion, slid his hand lower through the wiry tendrils, and she half screamed as his hand touched the edge of the dark entrance. "Yes, God, yes," Dulcy cried out, and her torso rose, the portal of all portals offering itself. He felt her hips quiver as her torso lifted, stayed, waited, and he brought his pulsating warmth to her, touched, stayed, and Dulcy screamed as her lean legs slapped against his hips. "Yes, yes, yes . . . aaaaah, yes," Dulcy groaned, despair mixed with desire in her voice.

He slid forward and felt the warm wetness of her flowing around him, eternal welcome, and she was uttering tiny panting sounds, half grunts and half cries, exhortations of ecastsy as her legs pulled tight against him, pushing him deeper inside her. Her cries rose, became screaming moans as he slid deeper, drew back, slid forward again, and then she was pushing and pulling with him, every part of her welded to him, her breasts hitting into his chest as her body rose and fell, bucked and jerked with an overwhelming frenzy. He was, he realized, a captive, overcome, caught up in the demanding fury of her pure ecstasy, and her small half screams against his cheek were entreaties for more. She suddenly somehow swung hips, and in moments she was atop him, bucking furiously, driving herself as deep and hard as she could onto him, her face falling down against his, her mouth crushing his as tiny sounds escaped her lips. The word *possessed* came to him as she rode him with an explosion of ravenousness, almost a rapacity of pleasure.

"Oh, God, yes, yes, yes," Dulcy screamed as she plunged and bucked and plunged again and flung her breasts down onto his face. Suddenly, he felt her slam down against his groin with an extra measure of desperation, and he felt her legs grow tight against his hips, and then he could feel the spiraling contractions of her against his own pulsations. "Now, now, now . . . Jesus, now," Dulcy screamed, and her cry was a shattering sound that spiraled in rhythm with her inner, throbbing contractions, and he felt himself swept away with the total, consuming ecstasy of that trembling moment. Dulcy clung to the last precious instant of her absolute ecstasy, and only when her final cry broke off in midair did he know that the consuming totality of Dulcy's passion had torn itself apart. "God, oh, God," Dulcy murmured despairingly as she fell atop him, all of her limp, only the soft throbbings inside her still remaining, tiny afterthoughts of the flesh, and finally she lay still. He stayed, letting her move first, and when she pushed herself back, she fell onto her side against him. He looked over at the pale-fire blue eyes and saw a tiny, almost mocking laughter in them. "What was it you said about not caring?" she murmured.

"I've been wrong before," he said and smiled.

She pressed herself to him. "You were something special. I don't want you to leave when this is over, and I've never said anything like that to anyone before. She began to draw a slow line with her lips across his torso, down over the flat muscles of his abdomen, continued the slow invisible path down further. "I'll make it so you'll never want to leave," she murmured and added actions to words with an almost soundless yet no less frenzied plunge into pleasure. Finally, she lay against him again, limp with satisfaction, the veiled smile in her pale-fire eyes again. "Enough caring for one night?" she murmured.

"I'd say so," he agreed, and his eyes moved across the lovely leanness of her, lips slightly parted, breasts still rising and falling as she drew in slow gasps of air. But as he silently admired her, he reminded himself that there was a difference between passion and caring. Dulcy certainly had the first, but he was still not satisfied she had the last. As he closed his eyes to sleep beside her, he knew the question would stay tucked away in a corner of his mind. She would remain a fascinating enigma.

When morning came, she proved that again as she wrapped her arms around him after they finished coffee.

"I meant everything I said last night. You're really special," she said.

"Special enough to do things my way?" he slid at her.

She peered at him as a tiny furrow touched her brow. "Such as?" she asked.

"Let Paula go now. Words are words. Show me you really mean them," Fargo said.

The furrow grew deeper as she continued to study him. "That means you don't believe I'll keep my word," she said.

"No. It means I'd like knowing Paula is free," Fargo said.

"And I like being believed," Dulcy said, and he saw the hurt in her eyes. He swore inwardly and realized he hadn't expected that. Again, she proved a creature of unpredictability, and he turned a warm smile on her.

"You're still a good poker player," he said, and she returned the slightly smug little smile he was getting to know perhaps too well. A lot better than he knew Dulcy, he added silently. "I'm going to pay another visit to the castle. Roy knows I was at the Crews' place. Barlow saw me there," Fargo said.

"Yes, it's important you keep a line open to Roy. It could be your best chance to get Amy, and that's what comes first, last, and foremost," Dulcy said and went with him as he saddled the pinto. 'I'll expect you back tonight?" she said when he finished.

"Most likely," he said. "But don't get worried if I don't show. I may come onto something after dark." Dulcy gave him a lingering kiss, lips that echoed the night before and then stepped back to let him ride away.

He held a steady canter, alert for Indian pony trails, until he entered the canyon, where he increased his pace, rode down the center of the rich, heavily covered depression, and came to the incongruous structure that rose up near the west end of the land. The drawbridge was down, an the three guards watched him walk the horse across it and into the outer court. Roy Averson came out to greet him, Barlow at his side. "You're visiting everyone, I hear, Fargo," Averson said, a slight edge in his voice. "Not checking up on me, I hope."

"Didn't know there was anything to check up on," Fargo said smoothly.

"There isn't, but Dulcy could be filling you with all kinds of wild tales," Roy Averson said.

"I don't believe much of what I hear," Fargo said.

"That's good. We've a nice relationship, Fargo. You delivered everything I expected of you. I'd hate to see her ruin that."

Fargo kept his tone casual, his words the ones he had been contemplating during the ride through the canyon. "Truth is, Dulcy's only interest in me is if I can get Amy back for her," he said.

Roy Averson let a hearty laugh rumble from his chest. "I see you've come to know her. Just tell her there's nothing you can do to get Amy. Walk away from her. She's only trouble," the man said.

"I don't like to turn away from a chance at some real money," Fargo said. "She'd pay me real well if I could work out something with Amy."

"Work out something?" Averson frowned.

"I was thinking maybe I could talk you into some kind of arrangement with Amy. I'd split whatever she gives me with you," Fargo said with bland openness.

"What the hell are you talking about, mister?" Averson frowned.

"I was thinking something like you keep her half the

year and Dulcy the other half. She is the kid's mother, and I've a soft spot for mothers," Fargo said.

"You've a soft spot in your head, Fargo," Averson shot back. "Amy stays right here with me. Dulcy's a mother from hell, I told you. You let her worm her way into you and you're a fool."

Fargo shrugged and let himself seem apologetic. "Just a thought," he said. Anything further was cut off by Amy's voice, and Fargo glanced upward to see her head leaning from a window in the right wall of the keep.

"Where's Mrs. Stort. I'm hungry," Amy called.

"The fire went out in the kitchen, but she's got it going again. She's making your breakfast now," Roy Averson called up to Amy.

"She's a stupid woman. You ought to get rid of her," Amy said.

"I'll bring a tray up to you in a minute," Averson said, and Amy pulled her head in from the window. Fargo let his gaze stay on the window a moment longer. He knew where Amy's room was now, noting the location. Returning his eyes to Averson, he allowed a half smile.

"No wonder Amy's happy here. She gets the royal treatment from you," he remarked.

"She's happy here because she can't stand the way Dulcy treats her," the man answered.

Fargo gave a half shrug. "It seems you're busy now. I'll come back another time," he said. "I still think it'd be best for Amy if she could see both of you. A child needs a mother. I'd like you to think about it more."

"I always keep an open mind, Fargo, but it's not much open on this. But you come visit again. I enjoy visitors. I always like to hear the other fellow's view," Averson said, turned, and strode into the castle. Fargo smiled to himself. Roy Averson hoped to use him to perhaps find out Dulcy's thinking. Fargo felt Barlow's eyes boring into him, and he turned to the man.

"Roy's too goddamn nice to people," Barlow growled. "He thinks he ought to be that way."

"Behavior befitting the lord," Fargo said.

"Somethin' like that," the man grunted. "Now, me, I wouldn't give you the time of day, Fargo. I don't trust you."

"I'm real upset about that," Fargo said evenly.

"You will be, you keep coming into the canyon," the man threatened.

Fargo tossed him a deprecating smile as he swung onto the Ovaro and felt the man's glower. "Till next time," he said as he walked the horse across the drawbridge. The three guards there were still incongruous figures against the castle backdrop as they watched him go, and Fargo cast a glance back through the gate to the window of Amy's room, marking it again in his mind. But scanning the castle again also told him another incongruous truth. Six-guns, rifles, and modern firearms would have little effect on Roy Averson's re-creation of the Middle Ages. The castle and its defenders would remain as formidable as if they were in medieval times, perhaps more so, he mused grimly. He pushed aside the unhappy thought as he turned the horse west and rode to the other end of the canyon.

He made a wide circle, then slowed to take in the ranches and farms that he saw, returning the waves of some who greeted him from their plows. He came to halt at one place, where he saw four large barns and a half-dozen wagons in the open in various states of disrepair. As he approached the spread, he saw one barn held a smithy's forge, bellows, and a well-stocked toolshed alongside it. A man came from inside the barn, tall with a black, bushy beard, black hair, and an affable, ruddy face. Two younger men stepped from one of the nearby barns.

" 'Afternoon," the man called. "You're the feller that stopped at Henry Crew's place."

"Word gets around fast," Fargo said.

"Henry mentioned that Ovaro of yours. I'm Bill Ulrich. These are my sons, Rick and Don," the man said. A woman with graying hair pulled back and a lined but still attractive face came from the house. "My wife, Dorothy," Ulrich said, and Fargo swept the barns with a quick glance.

"You've a lot of equipment here. You the smithy for the canyon folks?" he asked.

"That and a lot more. I can make anything or fix damn near anything, wagons, plows, rakes, pitchforks, you name it. I hope one day I'll be attracting folks from outside the valley. For now, we try to be self-sufficient here," Ulrich said.

"Under Roy Averson's thumb," Fargo commented and saw Bill Ulrich's face tighten. "You in his grip like all the others?" Fargo questioned.

"Mr. Averson gave me the money to get all this equipment. Until I pay it back, he calls all the shots. I'm afraid there's no other way about it. It was a lot of money. Might be that it'll be Rick and Don who'll eventually pay it off," the man said.

"What if there was another way?" Fargo asked.

"I'd take it. So would everybody else. But there isn't," the man said, and once again Fargo felt the resignation of those who'd been broken in spirit.

"We'll see," he said, tipped his hat to Dorothy Ulrich and moved the pinto on. He left not wanting to hold out hope when he had none to give, yet convinced they needed some reason that would keep hope from dying out completely. It was late afternoon when he reached the Crew place and saw Loretta coming from the house, exuding the same combination of girlish, untouched prettiness and quiet maturity.

"Hello, Fargo," she said as he dismounted. "Been thinking about you, hoping you'd come by," she said, and Fargo let an eyebrow lift. She stepped closer, and he took in the sweet loveliness of her in a red-checked shirt and a black skirt that clung to long thighs. She brushed back her long brown hair with a gesture that was at once innocent and sensual, and he saw the deep, liquid-brown eyes studying him.

"Where's everybody?" Fargo asked.

"Gone to the Wilsons. They'll stay till tomorrow," Loretta said.

"No stomach for being here when the lord's man comes for you?" Fargo said, not hiding the disdain in his voice.

"Yes, but I understand," Loretta said.

"I don't," Fargo bit out.

"They can't help. They can only be hurt more," she said. "I told them to go." She stepped closer, and a tiny smile, almost wistful, touched her lips, and again she was that strange combination of innocence and maturity. "I told you I was hoping you'd come by," she said. "There is something you can do for me."

"Stand up for you? My pleasure. I'd love to shove the lord's privilege down his lordly throat," Fargo said.

"Not that exactly but kind of related," the girl said, and Fargo's frown questioned. "I want you to take me, completely. Fuck me, no holding back. That's what I want."

He stared at her and searched for words, but didn't find any.

5

Her liquid-brown eyes stayed on him, but no pleading in them, no coyness either, only a steady, unwavering frankness, eyes that were full of doe-soft youthfulness and yet womanly maturity. Again, she was a strange admixture, he noted and wondered for a fleeting moment if unusual combinations were endemic to the women of the area, Dulcy popping into his mind. Finally, his voice returned to him as he continued to stare at Loretta. "Damn, you're serious, aren't you?" he said.

"Very," Loretta said. "It's the only way I can strike back at him."

"How's that?" Fargo queried.

"Suppose you stood up for me and sent Barlow running; are you going to stay here with me from then on?" She let the question hang in front of him and followed it with a sad little smile. "No, of course you won't. You'll have to go your way, which means Roy Averson will come get me again, at another time. But he won't want me if I'm not untouched. I won't mean anything for him then. I'll have the last laugh."

The frown clung to his brow, but he knew she was right about Averson. His privilege would be empty then, meaningless. "Why me?" he asked. "There have to be young men here who'd jump at the chance to oblige. I met Bill

Ulrich. He's got two young sons. There have to be others."

"There are plenty who'd like to be in bed with me, but not to defy Roy Averson. They'd be afraid of reprisals against their families. You're the only one with nothing to fear from Averson," the girl said.

"I guess that's as good a reason as any," Fargo said.

"It's not the only one," Loretta said, and the liquid-brown eyes peered into him. "Those others, they're not for me, at any time. But you, the moment I saw you, I knew you were the one I would take. Roy Averson might be the reason. You would be the pleasure."

"Some might say that's making the best of a bad deal."

"I'd say it's turning a bad deal into the very best one," she countered, and he laughed.

"I like that better. I'm honored," he said, and she folded her hand into his as she led him into the house and to her room decorated with sheets dyed soft colors, a wide bed against one wall. She turned to face him, and her eyes stayed on his as her fingers went to the top buttons of her shirt.

"Should I?" she asked. "Or do you want to?"

"You start. I'll finish," he said and watched as she slowly undid buttons until the shirt hung open. He reached out, gently slipped it from her shoulders, and drank in the beauty of her, long, slender neck, slightly thin arms and shoulders, but her breasts were round, almost pale, a sweet, youthful soft firmness to them, nipples very pale pink and small, freshly virginal, each surrounded by an equally pale pink circle. But there was no shyness in her eyes, instead he saw a kind of defiance, and he undid the bow on her skirt and slid it down, taking her half-slip with it and saw a torso youthful in its slenderness yet very womanly in its sensuousness. Her very flat abdomen and a small, almost flat triangle added to her picture of girlishness, yet her thighs were luxuriously full and utterly womanly. He saw a slight tremor go through her body as he shed clothes, and there was more than appreciation in the way she looked at his smoothly muscled body. Her eyes moved downward, and he heard her short gasp as he reached out, pulled her to him, and held her body against his.

She stayed against him, rigidly at first, but he held her firmly, and slowly the tightness of her began to diminish, and soon she was pressed against him with warm softness. Little short breaths came from her lips, and she moved, rubbed the almost flat little nap against him, and gasped. He lay down on the bed with her, keeping her against him, and she gave a tiny laugh of pleasure, the senses awakening. He let his hand touch one of the sweet, soft-firm breasts, and Loretta Crew gave a tiny gasp of delight and her hands came to grasp his shoulders. Slowly, his thumb passed across the small, flat nipple, and she gasped again, stronger this time, the sound wrapped in delight. When he brought his mouth down to her breast and ran his tongue over the smooth tip, she cried out, and her body half turned, then turned back, and he felt her hands tighten against him. He gently caressed the little pale pink tip with his tongue, circling it, bringing his tongue down across it, gently pulling with his lips, and as Loretta cried out, he felt the flat little nipple begin to grow, firm, rise under the touch of his lips. "Oh, my, oh, my . . . ooooh, so nice, so nice," she murmured, and he kept his mouth closed around her as he let his hand move down in a pathless exploration. He slid his hand across the almost concave abdomen, paused at the little vertical indentation, still caressing, and now Loretta was uttering a stream of cooing sounds.

Her slender body twisted against him when he reached the small, shallow nap and was surprised to find a surprisingly firm pubic mound. "Oh, ooooooh, God," she hissed as his hand slid through the shallow, soft hair of her tiny triangle and began to reach the very tip when he heard her voice rise, a new note in it.

"It's all right," he whispered to her, then let his hand stay unmoving for a long moment and slowly slide downward. Her cries rose again, and he held his hand in place and, with surprise, felt the warm dampness of her thighs as he looked at her. The liquid eyes were deep, fathomless pools, but a tiny smile edged her lips.

"Go on . . . go on," she murmured, and he let his hand cup around the very tip of the damp V, and Loretta half screamed, a cry that hung somewhere between alarm and anticipation, protest and desire. He touched deeper, to the edges of the liquescent lips. "Oh, God, oooooh, ooooh, yes, oh, yes," she breathed as her hands dug into his back. Her thighs came together, stayed that way, holding his hand in place as she made the little cooing noises. He paused, then gently touched again, deeper, and with a sharp gasp Loretta opened her thighs and her hips lifted. They stayed, her body twisting, her gasped cry made of protest wrapped in wanting.

He moved carefully, gently, caressing the soft moist lips, and Loretta sighed and cooed and half moaned, and he felt her hand come down to cover his, holding him in place as she made tiny movements, rubbing her softness against him. When he slowly drew his hand back, she cried out in protest, her hand still atop his. "No, no . . . stay, oh, stay," she begged, but he took her hand, brought it down to the warm, throbbing erectness, and closed her fingers around him. "Oh, oh . . . oh, God, oh, yes, yes, oh, God," Loretta exploded, holding him, tight at first; then the wisdom of the flesh in command, she began to move her hand, stroking, caressing as sounds of new wonder and new pleasures fell from her lips. He stroked the insides of her full thighs, rubbing across the damp, smooth flesh, and she grew more excited, her body twisting, and her hand fluttering around him.

He moved and brought himself over her, and she responded with her body, her hips lifting, the senses guiding her, nature sweeping aside inexperience, desire overcoming uncertainty. He brought himself to the moist portal, entered slowly, rested against the wet, soft lips, and Loretta half screamed, the new wonder in her voice again and she moved, offered, and he slid deeper. "Oh, oh God . . . go on, go on, go on," she breathed as her hands moved up and down his sides, clutching at his buttocks, clawing against his legs, hips, ribs. He felt the almost frantic mixture of ecstasy and alarm that coursed through her, the wanting that had to find its way over fear. He moved deeper, slowly, felt her soft walls clutch against him, tiny contractions as they gave way.

"Oooooooh," she cried out in a long, sighing sound, the threshold of wanting suddenly crossed, the power of passion overcoming all else, and suddenly she was moving with him, her lovely slenderness pushing forward and backward as he moved with her. "Oh, God, oh so good, so good . . . so wonderful," Loretta breathed, and her arms came hard around his neck and pulled his face down to the sweet young breasts. She moved one hand, cupped it around one breast, and offered it to his mouth even as she slid up and down with him, falling into the rhythm of new delights. The pale pink nipple was standing up, a surrogate flag, a tiny signal of new passions crying out. "Yes, yes, yes. More, more, more," she breathed against his face, her voice filled with the discovery of self, all the passions of the flesh released. He stayed with her, slowly increasing the speed of his strokes, and Loretta began to twist and thrust with sudden wildness. She gasped out entreaties, cried out for more, and he let the gentleness ebb, and she reveled in the change, matched his every movement, her hands made into little fists that pounded the bed.

Suddenly, her hips rose and held, her slender body trembling and her voice rose in a sharp cry. "It's happening . . . something, something, oh, God, oh God yes, yes, yes," she screamed as spasms of ecstasy shook her body. "Now, now, now," she screamed, and he let himself go with her and saw her head fall from side to side as she was swept with passions beyond her, pleasures she had never felt before, caught up in the overpowering majesty of the senses, the new wonders of undisciplined, hedonistic excess. When she suddenly stopped shaking and her slender body fell back onto the bed, he heard the cry that rose from her and knew she had discovered that disappointment she had never known before. "No, no . . . too quick, too quick," she protested, and he stayed with her, in her, let himself soothe and support with the special comfort she also had to learn.

Her arms encircled him, and she clung to him as he felt her tiny contractions still moving against his throbbing shaft. She moved, pressing her breasts harder into him, and he saw her open the liquid-brown eyes and stare up at him for a long moment. "Thank you," she murmured, finally.

"I think that's for me to say," Fargo answered.

"No, thank you for making it so wonderful," she said. "It could have been different. I know that." She pulled his head down, and her lips clung to his. Finally, she let him go and gave a little cry as he slid from her. He saw the little smile that touched her lips as she sat up on her elbows and looked girlishly lovely. "It's done," she said, and he nodded. "That doesn't mean it can't be done again," she said.

"There was a special reason for this time," he reminded her.

"I'll find another," she said.

"I believe you would." He laughed and lay down beside her. She was wrapped in his arms at once, and he watched her eyes close as she fell into a satisfied sleep. He dozed with her and woke often to drink in the sweet loveliness of her. She had thanked him, but he realized it was he who felt strangely honored, as if having received a precious gift. He held her close as she continued to sleep until he saw the day beginning to fade through the window. She woke as he rose and began to put on clothes. "We'll be having company soon, I'd guess," he said, and Loretta quickly swung her full-fleshed legs over the edge of the bed and pulled on clothes.

"I guess I didn't want to remember," she said when she finished. He followed her from the house, then sat on a log, and she sat close beside him as dusk slid over the scene. There was still part of the day clinging to the land when the horsemen came into view, five of them riding hard. He saw Barlow in the front as they rode to a halt, the man's bushy black brows frowning down on him.

"What're you doing here, Fargo?" Barlow questioned.

"Waiting," Fargo said.

Barlow turned his eyes on Loretta. "Let's go," he barked. "You'll ride with me."

"He doesn't want me," Loretta said, rising to her feet as Fargo stood up with her.

"What?" Barlow frowned at her.

"He doesn't want me," she repeated. "I'm not what he wants, not anymore."

"What the hell are you saying? He sent me. That means he wants you. You know that. Let's go," Barlow rasped.

"I've been taken," Loretta said calmly.

Barlow stared at her. "Say that again," he growled.

"Someone got to me first," she said.

Barlow's brows knitted together as he stared at her. "What are you trying to pull, girl? Nobody'd dare," he roared.

Fargo's voice interrupted, his tone almost casual. "I would. I did," he said, and Barlow's head swiveled to him. He stared at Fargo's quiet expression as his own face became a mirror of racing emotions—astonishment, first, uncertainty next, then disbelief turning into acceptance and lastly, rage. "You bastard. You goddamn son of a bitch," Barlow screamed.

"Tell his lordship to shove his privilege up his royal ass," Fargo said calmly. Barlow's thick lips quivered with fury, and his hand started to move toward his gun. "I wouldn't try that," Fargo said. "Dead men can't deliver messages." Barlow pulled his hand back as he had the sense to read the message in Fargo's ice-floe eyes.

"Maybe you can outdraw me, but the four guns behind me will get you," Barlow said.

"Maybe, but that won't make you any less dead," Fargo remarked.

Barlow's eyes narrowed at him. "You're not riding out of here without paying for this," he said. "I'm going to beat you into the dirt and show girlie, here, what a mistake she made. No guns, just you and me. Come on, show her what a big man you are."

Fargo turned the challenge over in his mind. He'd prefer sending Barlow back battered than dead. It might still leave a little room for dialogue with Averson, he pondered. He wanted to keep that door ajar if not really open. His eyes stayed on Barlow. "Guns, no guns, either way's fine with me," he said. "You first," he added.

Barlow dismounted, carefully lifted his gun from its holster, and let it drop to the ground. "Your turn," he said.

"Don't play me for a fool. Your friends, too," he said, and Barlow nodded to the four men. They stayed on their horses, but dropped their guns on the ground. "Much better. Now I won't have to worry about a bullet in my back," Fargo said. His glance at Loretta saw the fear in her face, and he tossed her a smile as he stepped forward. Barlow raised his hands and came toward him, and Fargo took note of the thick-necked build of the man. Fargo circled, paused, and Barlow shot a short left, a fast, hard blow that grazed the side of Fargo's jaw as he twisted away. Fargo grunted inwardly. Barlow had speed. The man came toward him, tried another short left, but Fargo blocked this one, then lashed out with his own left. The blow landed high on Barlow's temple, but with enough force to make him step backward.

"You're gonna wish you never opened your goddamn pants," Barlow snarled.

"You're going to wish you never opened your goddamn mouth," Fargo said and flicked out another left, a short jab. But Barlow had the quickness to pull his head sideways, and the blow only grazed his ear. The man circled, came in low, straightened, and threw a left and right combination with both speed and power. Fargo parried the blows, but had to give ground and ducked to avoid another short left hook. From a half crouch he threw a looping left that caught Barlow on the jaw, and the man grunted as he went backward. Fargo's follow-up right cross had lost some of its power as it landed with Barlow going backward, but it nonetheless sent him further backward. Moving quickly, Fargo came in low and stayed low as Barlow swung vicious roundhouse blows that grazed his head.

Fargo sent a short, hard left into the man's abdomen, and Barlow bent half over with the pain of the blow. His arms were lowered as Fargo's right cross came up and caught him on the jaw. The man went down with an expression of surprise and pain crossing his heavy face. He hit the ground, rolled, and shook his head as he came up on his feet in time to see Fargo's lunging left hook coming at him. He tried to twist away, but the blow caught him high on the cheek, and Fargo saw the spray of blood from the man's face. Fargo shot a quick left and a right uppercut, and Barlow went down again, one side of his face streaming red. But he had strength, and he pushed to his feet, came in swinging, throwing lefts and rights, and Fargo had to go backward as he blocked the blows. Finally, as Barlow paused for breath, Fargo shot a piledriver straight left that caught the man on the jaw and spun his head half around as he fell to one knee. Fargo's right hook slammed into Barlow, and the man went down, rolling on his side, almost under the feet of one of his men's horses.

"Gimme," Barlow breathed as he pulled himself to his feet, and Fargo saw one man on a horse reach into his saddlebag, bring out something, and toss it to Barlow. Only when Barlow spun around did Fargo see he held a morning-star, the medieval weapon of steel chain links with two spiked steel balls at one end. Fargo glanced at where the Colt lay on the ground and saw it was too far away to reach. Besides, if he tried, the four men would jump down to retrieve their guns and reach them first. Fargo let Barlow come to him, the man's face streaming blood down one side, his mouth twisted in a vicious snarl. He swung the wicked weapon as he advanced, and Fargo circled on the balls of his feet, muscled calves tense.

Barlow lunged, swung the weapon, and Fargo leaped to his left as the spiked steel balls whistled past his head. He tried to bring up a counterblow into Barlow's stomach, but had to fling himself sideways as the spiked balls swung in a half circle at the end of the chain. Twisting away, Fargo tried to come in low, then leaped aside again as Barlow swung the weapon in a flat arc and the vicious balls grazed his forehead. The man knew how to use the weapon and with a flick of his wrist sent the spiked balls sailing downward as they reached the end of the chain. Fargo felt one hit against the side of his head as he tried to turn aside and cursed with the pain of the blow. He flung himself forward, diving to the ground, but the second of the steel spheres crashed into the side of his shoulder, and he felt the spikes tear through shirt and flesh.

The pain shooting through his arm, he hit the ground, rolled, and saw Barlow bringing the morning-star around in a downward arc. The two deadly spiked balls hurtling down at him, Fargo had no choice but to raise his arms, and let bone and muscle take the terrible impact to keep a fatal blow from his head. He heard his own cry of pain as the weapon smashed into him, but somehow managed to curl his fingers around the chain. He pulled, using all his strength made desperate by pain and fury, and saw Barlow's burly body come forward off balance.

Fargo brought a knee up, and Barlow's belly slammed into it. With a gasp of breath Barlow fell onto both knees as Fargo, blood pouring from both forearms, pulled the weapon out of the man's grasp. He rolled, came up on his hands and knees, and saw Barlow regaining his feet. Using all the remaining strength in his bruised and bloodied arms, Fargo flung the chain and the spiked balls in a flat trajectory. His lips drawn back in a grimace, he saw the medieval weapon smash into Barlow, the chain curling around the man's neck as the two spiked balls smashed into the back of his head to stay there, imbedded. Barlow managed to rise to his feet, both hands clawing at the chain around his neck, his mouth open and his eyes bulging. Futilely, he tried to dislodge the spiked steel balls in the back of his neck, managed another three steps, and then fell forward, twitched convulsively, and finally lay still.

Fargo pushed to his feet, ignoring the blood that coursed down his arms, and walked to Barlow's lifeless form. He dragged the man to his horse, picked him up by the belt and the back of his shirt, and threw him facedown over the saddle. He stepped back and saw Loretta bringing the Colt. His eyes sweeping the four men as he took the revolver, he bit out orders. "One of you, pick up all your guns and ride," he said, then waited as a short-legged man collected the four six-guns while another took Barlow's horse by the reins. "Tell Averson how I managed to use his toy without any training in it. Ask if that makes me a knight," Fargo said as the four riders retreated with their grisly burden. He turned as Loretta pulled at his shirt.

"Come inside . . . quick," she said and led him into the house as the last of the day turned into dark. Lighting lamps, she put a sheet on the bed and had him lay flat as she took the torn shirt from him. In moments she was cleaning the wounds on his arms, washing him down and then swabbing on a thick ointment. "Comfrey, white willow bark, and wintergreen compress," she said as she wrapped both his arms in thin sheets of fabric. He felt the instantaneous soothingness of the salve and lay still as she drew his trousers from him. She washed his face with cool water and curled herself beside him. "I did not expect this. I thought he'd come, listen, and go back to report," she said. "I wouldn't have asked you if I'd known this would happen."

"You sorry?" he queried, and Loretta sat up and her face was very serious, but he saw a dancing light in her eyes.

"Yes, for two reasons," she said. "Because you've been hurt and because you can't make love to me again tonight." She gave him a slightly mischievous glance. "What are you thinking?" she asked.

"Like a duck to water," he muttered.

"Good teacher, good pupil," she said and took her shirt off and lay down across his chest, taking care to avoid his arms. He felt tiredness sweep over him and let himself go to sleep with her. He didn't wake till the morning sun came through the window, and he opened his eyes to find Loretta watching him, looking beautiful with only her skirt on. She had the bandages in one hand, and he looked down at his arms. They still hurt as he flexed his muscles, but the bleeding had completely stopped. "I washed and mended your shirt while you were asleep," she said as he swung long legs over the edge of the bed, and she came to him, pressing the sweet, soft-firm breasts into his chest.

"I'd best get dressed and be on my way," Fargo said. "Your folks will be coming back. It might be awkward if I'm here when you tell them what you decided on doing."

Loretta's lips tightened, and the liquid-brown eyes grew even darker. "They were going to stand by. They've no reason to criticize me, none of them. And my mother will understand," Loretta said, and Fargo found himself admiring the young girl who, he realized, had been very much a woman before their night together. "Will you be coming back soon?" she asked.

"It might be a quick visit," he said.

"I can wait for another time. I'll be patiently impatient," she said smiling, and he nodded appreciatively at the words as he swung into the saddle. He rode away and knew there'd be no putting aside thoughts of Loretta. She had turned out to be an unexpectedly special moment. But as he rode from the canyon, his eyes were once again sweeping the terrain for signs of Indian. He found fresh hoofprints, steered away from them, and finally rode through Big Dusty, passed the Northwest Savings Bank and rode on out of the town.

He wrestled with telling Dulcy about the night and decided there was nothing to be gained by it. Her understanding might not be there, her feelings perhaps hurt, and he didn't want that. But he let himself think that what happened might reach Averson, and once his initial anger passed, make him rethink his ways. Perhaps wishful thinking, Fargo admitted, but he clung to the thought as he considered his next approach to Roy Averson. He was still contemplating the possibilities when he reached Dulcy's place. She came out to greet him, looking coolly beautiful in a light green shirt and clinging black skirt. He saw the pale-fire eyes search his face. "I waited," she said.

"Sorry. I decided to see what Averson did with his men during the night," Fargo said as he dismounted.

"What'd you find out?" Dulcy asked.

"Some paid visits to the ranchers, others kept a tight guard at the castle," he said, the answer true enough, he told himself.

"I could've told you that," Dulcy sniffed. "Now what?"

"I'm thinking about the best way to pay another visit to Roy," Fargo said.

"I'm going to town. I want to see Ben Hopkins," she said.

"Who's he?"

"President of Northwest Savings," Dulcy said, and his eyes studied her.

"The payments for Amy come through the bank. You figuring on finding a way to disrupt them?" Fargo questioned.

"Go to the head of the class," Dulcy said. "There probably isn't any way, but there's no harm in trying."

"Guess not," Fargo thought aloud. "That'd give him a problem."

"Exactly," Dulcy said.

"You know this bank president well enough to do something like that?" Fargo asked.

"Been dealing with Ben Hopkins for years. He'll level with me if there's a way," Dulcy said.

"Something's been bothering me," Fargo put forward. "It's plain that Roy Averson isn't a man burdened by scruples. You've been a constant problem to him. I'm wondering why he just hasn't gotten rid of you."

"You think he can't bring himself to do in his own daughter?" Dulcy said with a grim snort.

"The thought occurred to me."

Dulcy's laugh was harsh. "That's not it. Aunt Clara made a provision in her will that I had to be alive and there for Amy until she was sixteen or the payments stopped. She knew Daddy dear all too well."

"So he can take Amy, but he can't touch you," Fargo said.

"Bull's-eye. No fatherly compunctions, just dollars.

I'm alive because he hasn't found a way to get around that yet," Dulcy said, the bitterness plain in her voice.

She was entitled to bitterness and anger, but Fargo found himself wondering if her answer applied in reverse. Was Roy Averson alive because she hadn't found a way to get around that yet? He felt slightly ashamed at the question and knew it was there only because he still saw too many similarities between them.

"Wait till I get back," Dulcy said, coming to him, suddenly all softness. "I missed you a lot." He nodded, and she kissed him, a long, promise-filled kiss and then hurried from the house. He sat down on the sofa and felt the pain still in his arms, but let himself relax and rest. There'd be time to go visiting Roy Averson. Perhaps it was all to the good that the man had more time to think about his own decisions. Fargo closed his eyes, stretched his long legs out, and dozed until the sounds of hoofbeats woke him. He rose and went to the door to see Dulcy swing from the horse and stride toward him, fury in the pale-fire eyes. "You stupid son of a bitch," she snapped, and he barely ducked away from her hand as it came around to hit him.

"You always change moods this fast?" Fargo asked as she swept into the house.

"When I hear what I heard in town," Dulcy said, ice coating her voice. "Some of the ranchers from the canyon were in town, talking about you and Loretta Crew. I didn't believe my ears, but then I knew they're not the kind to make up stories."

"She wanted me to do it," Fargo said. "It was her only way of striking back."

"And you were so goddamn willing to oblige," Dulcy hissed, and he was taken aback at the depth of feeling in her voice. He was touched, too, he realized.

"I hoped you might understand," he said.

"Understand? Why would I? Jesus, how could you, how could you?" Dulcy flung at him, and he felt a wave of contrition sweep through him.

"I did what I thought was right. I didn't mean to hurt you. I'm sorry you're this upset, I really am," he said.

Dulcy frowned at him. "Wait a minute. You think I'm upset because you screwed the little bitch?" she snapped.

"Well, I guessed so, listening to you," Fargo admitted.

Dulcy flung the words as though they were whips. "Don't flatter yourself. I don't care if you screw her every hour on the hour. I'm furious because you had an open door to Roy Averson, and now you've gone and closed it. Not only did you screw the damn girl, but you went and killed Barlow. How fucking stupid can you be?"

Fargo stared at her as her fury trampled the contrition he had felt. "I guess I was wrong about you being hurt. My apologies," he said.

"Don't be smart with me," Dulcy snapped. "How the hell do you plan to get Amy, now that you've slammed the door shut to Roy? How? Think about that, Mister Good Deed, and think about your friend Paula."

"Now, hold on," Fargo began, but Dulcy cut him off.

"No, Amy is all that counts. I didn't think I'd have to remind you of that, but it seems I do," Dulcy said, and Fargo stared at her, taken aback by the total change in her.

"What happened to my being special? What happened to the things you never said to anyone else?" he asked.

"You're a special disappointment. Change that and I'll change," Dulcy returned with icy rejection. Once again, he saw she could become another person. Once again, he saw she was fire and ice, soft cotton and cold steel, and he wondered which was the real Dulcy. Or was she two people wrapped in one, each equally real? He stared back into the pale-fire eyes, and she remained a beautiful enigma.

"I don't figure I've closed my door to Roy Averson," he said.

"That shows how little you know the man. He won't forget this, not ever," Dulcy answered.

"But he respects me, more than ever. He might even listen to me now," Fargo insisted.

"Even if he does, it won't mean anything," Dulcy sneered.

"I'll make it mean something," Fargo said.

"You don't understand how rotten he is," Dulcy said.

"You don't understand how smart he is," Fargo said, and Dulcy let disdain sweep across her face. "He has something going for him in the canyon. He doesn't want to see it ruined, and Roy Averson understands how much trouble one man, the right man, can cause him."

Dulcy's opaque eyes grew even more opaque. "Prove it," she said, challenge and doubt in her voice.

"I will, but you know something? You're making it damn hard for me to know if I'm doing the right thing for Amy," he threw at her.

She stepped forward, put her hands against his chest, and suddenly her voice was all softness. "I know," she murmured. "But you are. You'll know that in time."

He turned and strode from the house, cursing silently as he wondered again which side of her was the real one.

6

He bedded down on a carpet of nut moss alongside a stream and made plans before he let himself go to sleep. He woke with the new day, washed and dressed, then rode beside the stream. Only a few Indian pony prints met his eyes, and when he reached the base of the canyon, he passed near enough to the Crew ranch for Loretta to see him. She pulled herself onto a wide-backed plow horse and rode out to meet him. The girlish sweetness was still very much part of her, but he saw a new wisdom in the tiny smile that edged her lips. Leaning over, she brushed his lips with hers and then sat back, words unneeded.

He drew a sigh as he spoke. "I thought it would stay just between us a little longer," he said.

"When the others returned, I had to tell them why I hadn't been taken," Loretta said.

"Of course," Fargo agreed.

"I'm sorry if it caused you any trouble," she said.

"Dulcy was pretty damn mad," Fargo said.

"Jealousy? She was hurt?"

"No. I made the mistake in thinking that. She feels I cut myself off from reaching Roy Averson," Fargo said.

"She's probably right," Loretta said. "But what you did for me had a strange effect on everyone in the canyon."

"How?"

"It seemed to give them some pride, but at the same time make them more afraid of some backlash from Roy Averson," she said.

"I'll pay him a visit," Fargo said, and saw the alarm sweep through Loretta's face.

"Don't. That'd be like going into the lion's den," she said.

"Maybe. Then there are ways to tame a lion," he said, and her hand closed around his arm.

"Be careful," she said, leaned forward again and kissed him, a soft touch that ended as quickly as it began, and she turned the plow horse back to the ranch. He rode on and stayed close to the side of the canyon to let every one of the farmers and ranchers see him. Each one waved as he passed, and he kept a steady pace till he reached the castle. The guards at the drawbridge stiffened as he approached, but let him ride across without a challenge. He brought the horse to a walk as his eyes swept the drawbridge and made a mental note of the width of the moat beneath it.

Inside the court Amy groomed the Cob at one side, and a number of men worked at various chores. Averson had some thirty men, he estimated, perhaps as many as forty, and he rode to a halt and dismounted as Averson came out to meet him. Four men appeared to take up positions behind Averson. "You've a lot of brass, I'll give you that," Averson said.

"Didn't think you were a man to hold a grudge," Fargo said blandly.

"Hang onto that sense of humor, Fargo. You're going to need it," Averson growled.

Fargo paused and swore silently at himself before he answered. He hated the decision he'd made and felt both helplessness and shame at having to turn his back on the people of the canyon. But Paula had to come first. Dulcy held her over his head, and from Dulcy's icy fury he knew he couldn't expect compassion from her. He had little choice but to make his bitter bargain. "I'm here to make you an offer," he said to Averson. "You've got a good thing going for yourself here. You own the poor souls in the canyon, and I'm sure you want to keep it that way. You wouldn't want it to blow up in your face."

"I don't expect that'll happen," Averson said confidently.

"I can make it happen," Fargo said. "You know that." Averson's eyes narrowed, his silence a kind of admission. "It's simple. You give me Amy and you'll never see me again. You don't and I stay here and fuck up your whole operation. It's as simple as that, your lordship."

"That's how you see it, is it?" Averson asked.

"That's right," Fargo said. "And so do you."

Roy Averson's eyes stayed narrowed. "Suppose I think on it," he said.

"Till the morning," Fargo said.

"I won't need that long. I'll send you an answer by tonight," Averson said.

"Where?"

"You at Dulcy's?" the man asked.

"I can be."

"You wait there," Averson said.

"Good enough," Fargo said, climbed onto the horse, and began to back the Ovaro toward the gate, one hand resting on the Colt at his hip.

"I could have you blown away right now. It'd be simpler," Roy Averson mused aloud.

"You could, but you know I'd kill you before you finished giving the order," Fargo said, and Averson allowed a wry smile. Fargo backed the horse across the drawbridge onto the ground at the other end before he turned and rode away at a canter. He rode down the center of the canyon as the day began to slide toward an end, reached the mouth of the canyon, and emerged onto the high land. His eyes swept the ground for Indian markings at once, saw but a few, and continued on to pass through Big Dusty, where a somewhat portly man in a banker's frock coat was locking the bank door. The man glanced at him as he passed, and Fargo saw a slightly chubby face, the beginnings of a double chin, and very sharp blue eyes under pepper-and-salt hair.

He rode on, and the dusk was turning into dark when he arrived at Dulcy's place.

She came out at once, the opaque blue eyes searching his face. "You're alive and back. I guess that's an accomplishment," she sniffed. "But I don't see Amy."

"Don't be in too big a hurry," Fargo said as he swung to the ground. "He said he'd give me an answer tonight."

"He did?" she said with some surprise.

"That's right."

"I've cold chicken and potatoes. You can eat while you're waiting—while we're waiting," Dulcy said, and he went into the house with her. She came to him in the living room after he finished the quick meal and sat down close beside him, all the harshness gone from her face. "I'm sorry I get so angry, but that's how I am. I'm made of extremes," she said.

"That's for damn sure," he grunted.

A half smile touched her lips. "There'll be more of the ones you'll want to remember," she said.

"I'll try to keep that in mind," Fargo muttered.

She leaned over, and her mouth pressed his, wet and warm, her lips parted, tongue slipping out. She took his hand and brought it to one soft breast, then held it there tightly. "This will help you," she murmured.

"It will," he said laconically, and she kept his hand on her breast as she leaned back against him. He didn't pull away, enjoying the touch of the dark-red nipple between his fingers. She seemed perfectly content, her head on his shoulder and thoroughly relaxed, and once more he marveled at the total dichotomy of her. But he stayed, put his head back, and let time drift on. He half dozed in the comfort of her warm softness and allowed himself the luxury of feeling confident. Moments stretched out, became hours, when suddenly he sat up as the moon climbed higher into the sky, shining through the window. He leaped to his feet and Dulcy came with him, her eyes on him.

"Learning about Roy Averson's promises?" she asked.

"Learning about his cleverness," Fargo bit out as the words flooded back over him, Averson's first. *I'll send you an answer by tonight,* he had said. *You at Dulcy's?* Fargo recalled nodding. *Wait there*, Averson had said. Fargo turned the words over in his mind again, everything suddenly taking on a new, icy meaning. "Shit," he swore as he started for the dooorway. Roy Averson had tricked him, set him up, and he'd fallen for it.

"He lied to you about giving you an answer," Dulcy said.

"No, damn him. Nothing that simple. He let me think I'd get his answer here," Fargo threw back as he raced from the house and vaulted onto the Ovaro.

He sent the horse off at a full gallop, cursing Roy Averson's sneaking cleverness, as he rode through the darkness and down into the canyon. Keeping the horse racing at top speed, he kept hoping he was wrong, and the darkness stayed untouched until he turned east inside the canyon toward the Crew ranch. He saw the darkness torn apart then as an orange glow spread upward into the black night, and he heard himself shout in helpless rage. As he raced closer, he heard gunfire, then shouts and screams. When he reached the scene, he saw two of the barns in flames and Averson's men riding back and forth, shooting wildly. He reined to a halt, Colt in hand, and brought down the nearest rider with a single shot.

A ladder had been placed against the main house, and Fargo saw two figures on the roof, one, Averson's man trying to set the roof afire with a grease-soaked torch, the other, Loretta struggling with him. Fargo ran, saw another of Averson's men, and brought him down without breaking stride. He reached the ladder and pulled himself up the rungs to get to the roof just as the man sent Loretta sprawling with a blow. Clambering onto the roof, Fargo raised the Colt as the man turned. "Throw the torch off the roof," Fargo ordered as he half crawled, half pulled himself forward. "Now, dammit," he shouted. The man raised the torch and half turned as if he were about to toss it from the roof, when he spun and flung it in a low arc. Fargo saw the fiery end of the torch hurtling at him, threw himself flat onto the roof as the object passed over him, and he felt the searing heat of it. The man was charging, yanking his gun out as Fargo fired from his prone position on the roof. The shot caught the torch wielder in the stomach, and the man clutched both hands to his midsection, stumbled forward, and fell. He rolled on the slight slope of the roof, and Fargo watched him go over the edge, hands still clutched to his stomach.

Glancing up, Fargo saw Loretta on her feet, stamping out little curls of fire that had caught on the roof boards and turning, he saw Averson's men still racing back and forth below. He also saw a figure lying on the ground, and he cursed silently as he fired and saw two of the riders fly from their horses. He pulled his head back from the edge as an answering round of fire sent bullets smashing into the roofline. But the return fire stopped, and Fargo raised his head to peer down and see the riders galloping away. He pushed himself to his feet as Loretta reached his side and clung to him. "They just came out of the night," she said. "Shooting and throwing their torches. It was all so sudden," she said.

"Let's get down," he said and helped her climb down the ladder. He went with her as she hurried to where Emma Crew had helped her husband to a sitting position.

"Took a bullet in the shoulder," Harry Crew said. "But I'll be all right. It passed clean through."

"I'll get him to the Offermans. We'll stay there tonight," Emma Crew said as she helped her husband get to his feet.

"I'll be along later," Loretta said, and Fargo saw Harry Crew and his wife scan the still smoldering ruins of their barns.

"Thank God they didn't burn down the house," Harry Crew said.

"They would have if Fargo hadn't gotten here," Loretta said, and Fargo saw the man peer at him.

"How'd you know?" Crew queried.

"I thought I'd made a deal with Roy Averson," Fargo said, unwilling to put his devil's bargain into words. "I suddenly realized he'd tricked me. The rest was easy to put together."

Harry Crew's face turned bitter, his mouth tightening. "This was his answer to what you and Loretta did," the man said.

"Only in part," Fargo answered. "He was saying more to me."

Harry Crew's eyes turned to his daughter. "Still think you did any good for us?" he said accusingly. "Seems all you did was satisfy yourself."

"That's not fair," Fargo cut in. "She stood up for herself when none of you would. You were all holding your heads up a little higher afterward."

"Nobody'll be holding their heads up now," the man muttered as he walked away with his wife. Loretta at his side, Fargo watched them climb into a buckboard that had escaped the fire and drive away.

"He's right," Loretta said softly, and Fargo swore inwardly at the bitter truth of her words. A moment of hope had come their way. Self-respect had stirred. Spirit had reawakened. But with one move, Roy Averson had snuffed out the flickering spark that had flared. He hadn't simply given his answer. He had seized the time to send a message. Fargo felt anger spiral inside him as he turned to Loretta.

"I won't give up on them, and I won't give in to him," Fargo said, and Loretta offered only a rueful shrug. "Not just words. I'll find a way to stop Roy Averson," he added. Her rueful smile stayed as she took his hand and led him into the house, where he found himself in her room. She pulled open buttons as he watched.

"There may not be another time, and I've thought only of the last time," Loretta said as she stood before him, beautifully naked, the pale pink nipples still flat and sweetly virginal. But in the way she faced him he saw a new note, a quiet boldness that echoed the newness of her womanhood. He shed clothes as she put her arms around him, and in moments he was holding her against him on the bed, letting her hands explore his muscled body. "Oh, oh yes . . . aaaaah," she said, finding his already swollen maleness, her cry one of delight and discovery. He let her have her way, enjoy her every discovery, revel in her own delight and in the pleasure she gave him. She was a child returning to newfound delights and a woman enjoying all the senses of womanhood. When he brought himself to her, she was waiting with anticipation, her body moving with a freedom and abandon newly found. "Yes, oh, God, yes, yes, yes," Loretta cried out as he filled her, and she surged with him, held his mouth to the pale pink tips, and clasped her full-thighed legs around him. She entered with newfound delight to all the sensual awakenings that proved even more rewarding than the first time. Finally, the moment came when she screamed and trembled and exploded with him. She found that pinnacle of pleasure again, no longer new, yet forever new, making her understand again the meaning of her self.

She lay with him afterward, murmuring in protest when he finally drew from her, and he lay with her and waited until she emerged from the half sleep of senses completely satisfied. She rose on one elbow, her liquid-brown eyes holding pain. "I want you to forget about us, Fargo. We must live with what we let happen," she said.

"You're sounding like Dulcy," he said.

"It's true. You tried. You did what I asked of you. But it is not your problem. Don't risk your life any further," Loretta said.

"It's not just for you," he told her. "I'll be going up against Roy Averson for other reasons that don't really concern you, so I might as well include you in, all of you."

Loretta's eyes took on new sadness. "You can't give them what they've abandoned, will, spirit, courage," she said.

"It was in them once. It can be rekindled. As I said, I'm

not giving up on them or giving in to Roy Averson. I can't," he said.

She folded herself tighter against him. "If there is a way, I'm sure you can find it, only you," she murmured and let sleep sweep over her. He closed his eyes and slept with her until daybreak when he rose, washed, and dressed. He was standing at the window when Loretta woke, pulled on a robe, and stood beside him as he saw four horsemen appear along with an open light delivery wagon. "What do they want here?" Loretta asked.

"Burial squad, come to pick up their people," he said and watched the men lift the bodies into the wagon. He went outside when they finished and enjoyed the nervous glances the men threw his way. "Where's Averson?" he asked.

"Out riding with the kid," one said.

"With Amy?" Fargo echoed in surprise.

"She won't stay cooped up in the castle," the man answered. "She insists on getting out."

That figured, Fargo commented to himself as the men drove away with the wagon and he returned to the Ovaro. Loretta came outside to him at once. "When will you be back?" she asked.

"Soon enough," he said and climbed onto the horse, waving back as he set off at a fast canter. He swung wide to avoid the wagon, found a low rise in the land, and stayed on it as he moved toward the canyon. He rode perhaps ten minutes when the land dipped and he saw the knot of riders directly ahead. He squinted and picked out Amy on the Cob as she rode back and forth through a field of wild geranium. He counted eight horsemen on guard in a rough half circle, then found Averson off by himself as he watched. He spotted a stand of white fir, entered the trees, slowed the horse to a walk, and came out only a dozen yards behind where Roy Averson watched Amy ride. "Don't do anything stupid," he said, his voice low but with enough power in it for Averson to hear.

Averson slowly turned in the saddle to look back at him, and Fargo saw the icy satisfaction in the man's face. "Got my answer, I hear," Averson said.

"I did," Fargo said and drew a deep breath. He hated making decisions in which he didn't have a lot of confidence. Yet he had to try for one more answer, one that would tell him things he had to know, an answer that would decide his next moves. But not from Roy Averson. "Get Amy over here," he said.

Averson's brow furrowed as he stared back. "You crazy?" he asked. "My men have orders to shoot if anyone touches her. You won't get six feet with her."

"Don't figure to run off with her," Fargo said. "You're not going to risk shooting a little girl coming along peaceably, are you?" Averson didn't reply, but his frown grew deeper as he stared back. "Now, get Amy over here," Fargo said.

Averson waited another moment, and Fargo cursed inwardly as he saw the contemptuous smile move across the man's face. "You are crazy," Averson said.

"Get her over here before my trigger finger acts on its own," Fargo growled.

Averson turned to the child. "Come over here, Amy," he called, and Fargo watched the child ride over on the Cob. She came to a halt, her eyes on him, full of unsmiling, cool curiosity.

"Hello, Amy," Fargo began. "Your mother wants to see you. She sent me to fetch you."

"She can come visit anytime here," Amy said. "Roy has said so over and over."

"She doesn't want to visit. She wants you back with

her. She misses you very much. She's your mother. You belong with her. Don't you miss her?" Fargo countered.

"I'm happy here," Amy said, cool dismissal in her voice.

"I'm afraid that's not everything, Amy," Fargo tried.

"It is to me," Amy returned, her child's face not at all childlike. Fargo cursed under his breath, Amy's answer not only made of very adult finality, but terribly revealing. Roy Averson's voice, wrapped in smug triumph, echoed the thoughts that hung in his mind.

"You lose, Fargo. It's not my doing. Amy's a little girl who knows what's best for her. She makes her own decisions," the man said, perhaps with more truth than he realized. "Now, you be a smart boy, Fargo. Ride out of here and keep riding. This is my world here, and there's nothing you're going to do to upset it."

"Maybe you're right," Fargo said and saw Averson's condescending smile. "Then maybe you're not," he added, and the man's smile vanished. Backing the Ovaro into the trees, Fargo disappeared into the foliage and heard Averson shout orders to his men. The sound of hoofbeats at a fast canter followed immediately, and Fargo kept the Ovaro at a walk through the trees. He found a particularly thick stand of the firs, halted, slid from the saddle, and took the big Henry from its rifle case. He crouched inside the dense foliage, waited, saw two of the riders moving through the trees, then another pair behind them.

He raised the rifle and took aim at the nearest rider as the man slowed. Though his target was partially obscured by the foliage, Fargo's finger tightened on the trigger as he fired a single shot. The man screamed in pain as he managed to avoid falling from his horse. The others turned their mounts, firing off three wild shots in alarm.

Fargo considered firing again when he heard Roy Averson shouting orders and his men began to retreat from the woods, pulling the wounded rider along with them. Fargo lowered the rifle as he rose to his feet, a thin smile on his face. Averson's instant reaction had sent a message he didn't intend to send. It said that having his men picked off particularly angered him. It was an irritation that could be used, Fargo made note.

Returning the rifle to its saddle case, Fargo climbed onto the Ovaro and rode from the forest. He kept a leisurely pace as he let thoughts arrange themselves in his mind, and when he reached Dulcy, he had formed plans. She came out to meet him, her pale-fire eyes narrowed as they studied him. "It wasn't good," he said.

She uttered a wry sound. "Didn't expect it would be."

"I tried to reach Amy. Didn't get anywhere," Fargo said.

"Of course not. She's under his influence there," Dulcy said. Fargo didn't answer, but he knew her words were but a half truth. Little Amy was her own master, more so than most adults were.

"I've been thinking about Averson and the ranchers," Fargo said.

"What?" Dulcy interrupted, a frown darkening her brow. "Forget the goddamn ranchers. You concentrate on Amy."

"It all hangs together," Fargo said.

"How?" Dulcy shot back angrily.

"I have to get to Averson before I can get to Amy. I have to make him see that he's no longer in control, that he doesn't have absolute power anymore. Only then can I get to him on Amy," Fargo said.

"And how do you expect to do that?" Dulcy almost sneered.

"By keeping him off balance, by showing him he's far from invincible, and by breaking his hold on the families in the canyon."

"You can't do that. You saw that yourself. They won't go against him. They're too afraid."

"They would if they weren't in his grip anymore," Fargo said.

"But they are," Dulcy protested.

"I think I know how to change that," Fargo said, and Dulcy's frown stayed. "But I'm going to need your help. You said you've known the president of the bank for years."

"Ben Hopkins? Yes."

"You know him real well?"

"Well enough," Dulcy said. "He's always liked me, if that's what you mean."

"Then I want you to get him to cooperate. I want him to arrange a loan for every one of the families in the canyon so they can buy off Roy Averson," Fargo said. "I'll get them to put up their lands and valuables as collateral."

"You think they'll agree to do that?"

"Yes. They'll still be in debt, but it'll be to the bank. They'll be free of Roy Averson. They won't be his serfs anymore. His power over them will be broken. Once that's done he won't be Mister Big anymore, not to anyone. I say they'll jump at the chance."

"Why would the bank?"

"This'll be a package deal, the kind that appeals to bankers. But you'll have to get your friend Banker Hopkins to go along with it," Fargo said and leaned forward. "You won't be doing it for the ranchers. You'll be doing it to get to Amy."

Dulcy's eyes studied him, and he could almost hear the

questions turning in her mind. "That land's real valuable. Ben Hopkins would hold the notes to every piece as collateral?"

"Right," Fargo said.

Dulcy's eyes narrowed. "I like it," she said slowly. "Yes, I like it."

"A vote of confidence?"

"I wouldn't go that far," she said quickly. "But I'll talk to Ben. The bank might just go for it."

"I'll talk to the ranchers, after I make Averson a little more nervous. You just convince the bank to make the loans," Fargo said. "I'm sure you can do that."

She looked out at the dusk. "You staying?" she asked.

"No, I'll be back tomorrow. I've got to start keeping Roy Averson off balance, keep him on edge," he said, and Dulcy came to him, pressing her hands against his chest.

"I'll be especially grateful if all this works," she said.

"Enough to let Paula go now?" he slid at her.

"You know that answer," Dulcy said coldly and stepped back.

"Just thought I'd try again," he said and walked from the house, finally certain that the contrasts that were Dulcy were too deep to change. He took the pinto and rode away into the new night, kept a slow pace, and passed through the mostly darkened streets of Big Dusty. Slowing further, he passed the bank, the key to the success of his plan. A lone light burned from inside as he rode on, and he put down the temptation to stop. Dulcy would do a much better job of convincing Banker Hopkins to agree to the loans than he could, Fargo reminded himself. When he rode from the town, he kept the slow pace, and when he entered the canyon, the moon had climbed high in the sky. When he finally came to a halt, the castle rose up in front of him, a dark and brooding mass of stone, a misplaced symbol that had brought with it all the wrongs of another time.

He took the Ovaro into a thicket of bur oak, left the horse tethered to a low branch, and went on alone, the big Henry in one hand. He dropped to the ground and began to crawl the rest of the distance to the castle. The drawbridge was up, he saw, the moat surrounding the dark structure. But Roy Averson wouldn't rely on the moat alone. He was too careful for that, and Fargo crawled to the edge of the moat, stayed on his stomach, and let his eyes move up and down and across the castle walls. He paid most attention to the tall, narrow, vertical spaces called embrasures, letting his eyes move from one to another. Suddenly, he halted at one where he saw a figure appear. He put the rifle to his shoulder, waited as the figure stepped back, and then reappeared again. Firing a single shot, he saw the figure fall backward and vanish from sight.

Crawling backward, Fargo stayed low until he was away from the moat when he pushed to his feet and ran in a crouch as he heard the shouts from inside the castle. He reached the oaks, climbed onto the waiting horse, and rode away. It was all he'd wanted to do—irritate Roy Averson, keep him on edge, let him know there was no such thing as invincibility. A first step. There'd be others.

7

He bedded down in the canyon in a cluster of red ash and when morning came, washed and dressed beside a small stream. He returned to the tree cover after he spotted a patrol of six of Averson's men riding in an erratic pattern. They'd been sent out searching for him. Fargo smiled and stayed hidden in the trees until they went their way. When he left his cover, he rode out, his eyes picking up the trail of the six riders. He followed, hung back, saw the trail pause at three of the ranches, and then go on until it circled back to the castle. He watched as the men rode into the castle, and following a long line of hackberry, he circled the castle until he halted at the rear.

Averson had had embrasures built into the corner turrets and the front wall but not in the rear. As Fargo surveyed the back of the castle from the trees, he saw that the stone work there was considerably cruder than at the front, the stones not smoothly set against each other. With no embrasures for guards to shoot from and stones that could be scaled, particularly with grappling hooks, the rear of the castle presented definite opportunities. Averson had cut corners in building his medieval replica. He'd pay the price for that, Fargo muttered as he retraced steps inside the trees until he was facing the front of the castle again.

He studied the drawbridge over the moat and concluded there was no easy way to jam the mechanism to prevent it from being raised. He surveyed the castle and made mental notes of the placement of the embrasures in the corner turrets. Finally, his gaze halted at the entrance, where, peering through the open gate, he could see into the courtyard. Amy came into sight, washing down the Cob. She was alone with the pony. No one he could see was near her, and Fargo felt a thought explode in his mind. There was little chance he could pull it off, but the bold brashness of it would rattle Roy Averson to his heels. It would poke another hole in the aura of invincibility he used as part of his power. A wave of excitement surged through Fargo as he saw there were only two guards outside the gate.

He measured the distance from the tree line to the gate, concluding the Ovaro could cross it in some thirty seconds. Drawing the Colt, he flattened himself across the pinto's jet-black neck and sent the horse into a gallop. The Overo burst from the trees at a full gallop, its powerful stride devouring the short distance. The two guards had been casually lounging at the gate, and when they looked up, the Ovaro was at the beginning of the drawbridge. They never got their guns out of their holsters as Fargo's two shots sent both of them to the ground at once. He raced through the gate and into the court.

Amy looked up at the onrushing horse, her eyes widening in alarm. Out of the corner of his eye, Fargo saw other figures back deeper into the court whirl in surprise. But he was already leaning low in the saddle as he scooped up Amy with one arm. "No, let me go," she screamed as he brought her up to the saddle. He felt the power in her small fists as she struck him in the face. "No, put me down," she screamed again. But he held onto her despite

112

her struggles as he turned the Ovaro around to race back to the gate. But shouts, then shots, split the air, and he heard two bullets hit the ground near him, another whistle past his head. More shots exploded. They were shooting wildly. Averson hadn't appeared to stop them, and Fargo knew Amy could take one of the wild shots. He loosened his hold on her, let her slide down the side of the horse and drop to the ground as he raced on. He flattened himself against the horse again as two more shots whizzed over his head. He sent the pinto galloping from the castle, across the drawbridge, and onto the ground. He kept the horse at a gallop, slowing only when he swept into the trees, the shouts and shots following him from the castle.

Averson had reached the courtyard by now, he was certain, and he let a thin smile cross his face. Another thirty seconds, fewer wild shots, and he would have been able to flee with Amy, he realized regretfully. But Averson would remember, and that was important. It'd make him keep more of his men inside the castle, guarding Amy. That'd limit his freedom of action and make him think twice about sacrificing men in striking back. Slowing the pinto to a trot, Fargo rode away feeling satisfied. His next stop in the late afternoon sun was the Crew place, and Loretta hurried to him first as he dismounted. She was still against him when Harry Crew and his wife came from the fields behind the house.

"We know your heart's in the right place, Fargo, but we'd just as soon you didn't visit us again. You saw what your help brought us," the man said.

"Come anytime you want, Fargo," Loretta said.

"You see, you've even made my daughter disobedient," Crew said.

"I've helped her regain her pride. I'm going to do the

same for all of you," Fargo said. "I want you to bring everybody in the canyon here tonight, every one of the families."

"What are you expecting out of that?" Emma Crew asked.

"I'm expecting to let you hold your heads up again. I'm expecting to make you into men and women again instead of serfs. You just bring them all here," Fargo said.

"I'll bring them if they don't," Loretta said and kissed his cheek before he climbed onto the pinto and rode away. He kept a fast canter for most of the way, and when he reached Dulcy's place, he saw four of her men on guard, rifles in hand. He met her at the door as she opened it for him.

"Something happen?" he asked, nodding back to the guards.

"No, but I want to make sure it doesn't. What with all you're up to you might send Roy onto striking back at anyone," she told him. "I went to see Ben Hopkins," Dulcy added.

"That was my next question."

"It's a deal," Dulcy said and threw her arms around him.

"Good," he said when she pulled her lips from his.

"He's going to need the exact amount for each family so he can prepare the notes and the exact monies," Dulcy said.

"I'll have that tonight," he said. "I'll bring everything back to you."

"I'm keeping men on round-the-clock guard duty now, so don't come rushing in when you get back," Dulcy said.

"Good enough." Fargo nodded, turned the horse, and rode away as dusk began to descend. He stopped in at the saloon, and had a sandwich and a bourbon at the bar, from where he could see out the wide window. "You get a good view of the street from here," he said to the bartender. "Bet you see just about everyone passing by."

"When I'm not too busy, especially in the day," the bartender said.

"Guess you get to know most of the regulars around here?" Fargo asked, finishing his sandwich.

"Sure do," the barkeep said.

"You know Dulcy Washburn's hands?" Fargo asked casually.

"They come in regularly," the man said.

"They pass by regularly?" Fargo queried.

"Yes, one of her boys rides by every day, about midafternoon," the bartender answered.

"The same one?"

"No, but one of her hands comes by like clockwork," the barkeep said.

Fargo nodded, more to himself than the barkeep, paid for his meal, and went to the Ovaro outside in the dark of the new night. He reviewed his questions and the barkeep's answers as he rode. Nothing he'd asked had been out of idle curiosity. Events were moving quickly, events over which he might have little final control. He couldn't let Paula's life depend on so many unknowns, particularly when he harbored both mistrust and misgivings. Perhaps he was doing Dulcy an injustice. The thought had nagged at him, made him feel traitorous, but he'd decided to live with that. She was too much of an enigma, too unfathomable, too much a double person. So he had begun to make plans, quietly, inwardly, to hope for the best but prepare for the worst. His questions to the bartender had merely been putting those plans into more than thoughts.

He rode on with a kernel of bitterness inside him, but

mused about his plans until he found himself in the canyon and nearing the Crew ranch. They had cooperated, he saw, the yard outside their house crowded with wagons, mostly buckboards and farm rigs. A crowd spread out of their living room to fill the kitchen and entrance hall. He recognized a few, the Ulrichs, Jed Offerman, and Ben Bentley, but the others he'd not met, and he pushed his way through the crowd and found Loretta. She stood beside him as he surveyed the gathering. They all had one thing in common, eyes without any spark and faces that reflected quiet despair and defeat.

Loretta's voice cut through the murmur of voices, and the crowd became quiet. "This is Fargo. He has something to say to you that you'll want to hear," she said.

Fargo let his eyes move slowly over the tired faces. "I'm going to give you a chance to look in the mirror again," he said. "I'm going to give you a chance to get back your self-respect and take back your lives. That means getting you out from under Roy Averson."

"You got a magic wand, Fargo?" a voice asked.

"The next best thing. It's called money," Fargo said and saw the collective frown that spread across the room. "Roy Averson managed to put you in debt to him, so much debt that he owns you. Cross him, go against his demands, and he can call in his debt and make paupers out of all of you. But you know that, and you can't find a way out. There is one. I've arranged for a way each of you can pay off Roy Averson."

"With what?" someone questioned.

"With a bank loan enough for each of you to pay Averson what you owe him," Fargo said.

"You really mean that, mister?" someone else questioned.

"I sure do. You'll have to sign a note, put up your lands

and your belongings as collateral. You can't expect to borrow money without collateral. But you'll be free of Roy Averson. He won't have his hold on you anymore. Your note payments will be made to the bank, everything in proper business terms."

A bearded man rose, a thin woman at his side. "I went to Ben Hopkins once for a loan. I was turned down. How come he'll give us all loans now," he asked.

"This is a package deal. Bankers like that. It makes a more attractive item in their assets column. And there was a personal contact. Dulcy Washburn, she and Ben Hopkins are friends," Fargo explained.

"This also lets her hit back at her pa. We all know they hate each other," Ben Bentley said.

"I don't care about that. She's entitled to her reasons. I've got mine, and this sounds like the answer to all our prayers. Count me in," another man called out.

"Us, too," someone else said, and Fargo watched the others rise, almost as one, all murmuring agreement and all seized with a new excitement he could feel engulf the room.

"Each of you set down the amount you'll need to pay off Roy Averson. That way the money and each note can be tailored for each of you," Fargo said and heard the instant rustle of sound as they searched for scraps of paper on which to write. When they finished, Loretta collected each slip and handed them all to Fargo. "Don't breathe a damn word about this, not till we're ready to move," he told everyone.

"We understand," Harry Crew said.

"We'll meet here tomorrow night," Fargo said, and they all made their way from the house, suddenly very quiet. Loretta walked to the Ovaro with him as the others rolled away in their wagons.

"You've given them a new lease on life. It's a wonderful thing you've done," she said.

"Don't think I could've done it without Dulcy's help," Fargo said.

"She'll ask a personal price from you," Loretta said.

"Such as?" Fargo frowned.

"You never touch me again."

"Oh, no, that won't be part of it," he told her.

"You told me how angry she was about that," Loretta said.

"Only because it affected my contact with Roy Averson," Fargo said. "She said she didn't give a damn what I did with you." He saw an almost chiding smile slide across Loretta's lips. "You don't believe that," he offered.

Her smile stayed. "I know a woman's heart," she said softly.

He returned her smile. "Even though you've only been a woman a very short time?"

"Little girls know jealousy. Mark my words," she said.

He pulled her to him. "You're wrong on this," he said, and her lips clung to his until she stepped back, and then he pulled himself onto the pinto. He rode from the canyon as the moon began its path downward, found a spot near a stream, and bedded down. He drew a few hours sleep to himself and went on to Dulcy's place when the new sun rose. He found her dressed and looking beautifully cool in a deep yellow shirt and matching skirt. "This is all of it," he said as he handed her the slips of paper.

"I'll take them right to Ben," she said.

"I'd like to come along," he said.

"Why not?" Dulcy shrugged, and he went with her to the stable to get her horse, then took in the four rifle-toting guards along the fence.

"You'll be glad you helped arrange this," Fargo said to her as they rode from her place together. "Once Roy Averson knows he's no longer in power, that he has no more hold over anybody, he'll be a different man. A man stripped of his power is broken. He'll be willing to deal over Amy."

"What if he doesn't? I didn't do all this to play Good Samaritan," Dulcy sniffed.

"I'll find another way to get Amy," Fargo said. "But I won't need to."

"I hope not," Dulcy said, ice in her voice. They rode the rest of the way to town in silence, and when they drew up to the bank, Dulcy introduced him to Ben Hopkins. The man's slightly chubby face beamed, his pleasure at seeing Dulcy very obvious. "Dulcy's told me about the help you've been giving her," he said to Fargo, his blue eyes snappingly sharp.

Dulcy gave the banker the slips of paper. "It's all there, everything you'll need," she said.

"Good. I've the notes all drawn up. I need only fill in the names and draw the individual bank checks. It'll only take an hour or so. Why don't you two have some breakfast?" the banker said. "The Big Dusty Bed and Board is open."

"See you in an hour, Ben," Dulcy said and grasped his hand, holding on to it for what seemed longer than necessary to Fargo. When she left the bank, he walked beside her to the small breakfast room at the wooden inn.

"I'm glad we've this time to talk," Dulcy said to him over her cup of coffee. "I'm doing all this so you can get Amy, as you know."

"You told me you weren't playing Good Samaritan," Fargo said and nodded.

"Roy mightn't be ready to deal instantly. It could take him a while," Dulcy said.

"He might hold back some to save face," Fargo conceded.

"I want something from you meanwhile," Dulcy said. "Stay away from little Loretta."

Fargo kept the surprise from his face. "Didn't you tell me you don't care if I screw her every hour on the hour?" he reminded her, his voice bland.

"Changed my mind. It's a woman's prerogative," Dulcy answered. He smiled inwardly, Loretta's words swimming into his thoughts, testimony to the special power of female wisdom. He met Dulcy's waiting eyes, his gut reaction to tell her he'd sleep with whomsoever he damned pleased. But he decided not to irritate her at this time, his own plans already formed.

"Should I feel flattered?" he asked.

"Yes," she said and tossed him a quick, bright smile full of real warmth, and again he marveled at her split personality. When they finished breakfast and returned to the bank, Ben Hopkins was waiting for them.

"Here are the bank checks for each family. They sign the notes with each, and they can pay off Roy Averson. The monthly due date is on each note, everything strictly business. They'll be free of Roy Averson's demands."

"Exactly what we want," Fargo said. "I'll have the signed notes back to you in a day."

"Thank you, Ben," Dulcy said to the banker as she gave his slightly portly figure a warm hug and a kiss on the cheek. When Fargo returned to her place with her, he had the checks and notes in his saddlebag. "Satisfied?" she asked.

"So far," he said. "Except for Paula. I'd like her freed now." Dulcy's shrug was a dismissal, and he peered at her. "You ever think that I could've taken you off somewhere and made you tell me where you have her?" he asked.

"Beat it out of me?" she said with a half smile.

"That'd be one way."

"But not your way. We both know that," she said, and he swore silently at her instinctive knowledge of people. "Besides, I took that possibility into account," she said, and his brows lifted. "They don't get word every day by a certain time little Paula has had it."

He stared at her and realized he felt something close to a mixture of rage and grudging admiration. "You really are a piece of work, honey," he said. "You covered every angle."

"It's called playing your cards right," she said.

"I'll play the ones in my saddlebag," he said, and she watched him from the doorway as he rode away. He reached the Crew ranch at the beginning of dusk, and Loretta came to him after he dismounted.

"Some of the others are here already," she said, and he caught the sly probing in the glance she gave him.

"One for you," he grunted, and her little smile told him she understood. She studied him a moment longer.

"You going to follow orders?" she asked, and he caught the edge of cattiness in her tone.

"Dulcy's unpredictable. I'm not going to upset applecarts, not at this stage. There's more than you know about," he said.

"All right," she said, her hand finding his. The others arrived soon, wagons crowding around the house again, and Fargo took the notes and bank checks from his saddlebag.

"I'll call your names. Come up, sign the notes, and get your bank checks," he said, and a burst of applause traveled around the gathering. Jed Offerman stepped forward first, signed the note that put up his land as collateral, and collected the check. The others followed, each man, sometimes his wife also, signing the note for the amount needed to pay off Roy Averson. "We'll meet here in the morning and pay a collective visit to Roy Averson," Fargo said when they had finished signing.

"We going to need our guns?" someone asked.

"Don't expect any shooting, but bring them anyway," Fargo said. "And just the men folks."

"See you come morning," Bill Ulrich said and climbed into his farm wagon with his sons. Finally, Fargo stood with only Loretta beside him.

"I can't believe this has really happened," she said as he walked to the Ovaro. "Dulcy Washburn has her own reasons, we all know that, but I'm grateful to her for her part in making this come about."

"I think Dulcy could use a good deed or two in her knapsack," Fargo said.

"You sound as though you don't really like her," Loretta observed.

"Dulcy's a puzzle," he said.

She looked away for a moment. "I couldn't do that."

"Do what?" he frowned.

"Make love to somebody I didn't like," she said.

"Sometimes you don't know somebody until after you make love to them," Fargo said, not ungently.

"I'll take your word on that," she said, brushing his cheek with her lips and hurrying away. He climbed onto the horse and rode back through the night-filled canyon, ever alert for sounds, sights, and signs. The light was on in the living room when he reached Dulcy's place, and he walked the horse slowly and called out as he neared the house.

"It's me, Fargo," he said and saw two of the sentries step from the shadows, peer at him, and step back. Dulcy came to the door and let him into the house. "Here are the notes, all signed," he said.

She riffled the notes through her fingers, giving each signature a quick glance. "I'll bring these to Ben in the morning," she said, flashing a quick smile full of warmth. "It's going well. I feel very good about things," she said. "You can use the guest room for the night."

"I'd appreciate that," he said, and she saw him to the room, and he was strangely glad that she left at once. Her unpredictableness bothered him, he realized, more than it should. But he slept quickly, woke early, and rode back to the canyon and the Crew ranch. The others were waiting and formed a tight knot as they rode to the castle. Averson's men raced to the gate, rifles raised, as the group reached the drawbridge and reined to a halt. "Go get him," Fargo said gruffly.

"I'm here," a voice answered, and Roy Averson pushed through the crowd, surprise on his face as he took in the visitors. "What the hell is all this about?" he growled.

"These good folks have something for you," Fargo said, and Averson fixed him with a baleful stare.

"Where do you fit in?" Averson questioned.

"I made you an offer. You should've taken it," Fargo said. "Now I'm back."

"Let them in," Averson said and strode through the gate and into the courtyard, where Fargo saw another dozen men holding rifles. Amy's small, blond head looked out her window at him.

"Hello, Amy," he called out cheerfully.

"Forget Amy. What do you want here?" Averson barked.

Fargo turned to Jed Offerman. "You first, Jed," he said,

and the man dismounted and approached Roy Averson, reached out, and handed him the bank check. Averson frowned down at it.

"What the hell is this?" he growled.

"It's a bank check for everything I owe you, Mister Averson," the man said.

Averson was still staring at the check when Bill Ulrich and his sons stepped forward. "This covers everything we owe you," Ulrich senior said and stepped back. Another man came forward and handed a check to Averson, and the others followed in an uneven line until the last man has handed in his check. Averson's face was tight with fury as he swept the men with a disdainful glare.

"What's all this supposed to mean?" he asked.

"It means we don't owe you a red cent anymore, none of us," Harry Crew answered. "It means we're free men again. You haven't a damn bit of power over us anymore."

Fargo's voice cut in. "It means you're out of the lordship business, Averson. No more control over anyone. No more Mister Big. You're nothing. Empty. Zilch. And your castle's just a pile of rocks. It doesn't mean a damn thing anymore, and neither do you."

"Very clever, Fargo. But you didn't do this by yourself," Averson said.

"It was my idea," he said.

"You couldn't pull it off alone. Dulcy had to help you, damn her."

"She went along with it," Fargo said.

"I'll bet she did," Averson said.

"What's that supposed to mean?" Fargo frowned.

"You're not smart enough to see all of it. She's got something up her sleeve," Averson said.

124

"She felt sorry for the way you've been treating these good people, just as I did," Fargo said.

Averson made a contemptuous sound. "Dulcy never felt sorry for anybody. She's up to something," he said.

"Amy," Fargo said. "She figures now you might be reasonable about Amy."

"Go screw yourself," the man snarled.

"I'd think on it, Averson. The rules have changed. You're fresh out of power. Nobody has to pay any attention to you anymore. You can't squeeze anybody anymore, not for their money, their produce, their stock, or their daughters. I'd start being reasonable if I were you."

Averson's lips tightened into a thin line. His eyes held on Fargo, then swept the others in a steely glance. "I'd start thinking about how you're goin' to come crawling if I were you," he said, spun on his heel, and strode away. Fargo watched him go into the keep and then led the others out of the castle. After they'd left the drawbridge and rode down the center of the canyon, Ben Bentley spoke up.

"I don't like his answer," he said.

"Big talk. That's all he has left. You're all out of his clutches, and there's nothing he can do about that," Fargo answered.

"He's still got all his hands. He could come raiding and burning," someone said.

"That'd just be hitting back. It wouldn't change anything. He'd still have lost his power over you. But you might set up warning patrols just to be sure," Fargo said.

"We'll do that," Bill Ulrich said, and they halted where Fargo turned to ride east out of the canyon. "Thanks for all you've done," Jed Offerman said, and a murmur of agreement rose from the others. "Thank Miss Washburn for her part in it. We're real grateful for her help."

"I will. She'll appreciate that," Fargo said and rode on

after a round of handshakes. He felt satisfied, the warm feeling of having done something good curled inside him. It had been a beginning. Amy would be the finish, and he felt confident. Roy Averson had been hit hard and completely by surprise. His little world had suddenly been pulled out from under him. He was a self-made lord stripped of his power. He'd recognize that. He had no choice. Fargo set aside thoughts of Roy Averson, scanned the terrain for signs of Shoshoni as he rode, and finally arrived at Dulcy's place, where she waited in the doorway. "It's done," he told her.

"What about Amy?" she asked at once.

"It's too soon. I'll give him a couple of days to let reality sink in," Fargo said.

"You going to stay here and wait?"

"No. I'm going to keep checking on things."

"Things?"

"Roy Averson, the castle, his men, just in case," Fargo said.

"Make sure you don't include Loretta," Dulcy said. He smiled and wondered if she really did care or was just being bitchy. It was impossible to tell with Dulcy, he decided. Besides, he was just curious. He didn't give a damn whether she cared or not. He had no patience with enigmas, even beautiful ones. "When do I see you again?" she asked, cutting into his thoughts.

"In a few days, with Amy, I hope," he said.

"I'll be waiting," Dulcy said, and he rode away with his jaw set, bothered by her coldness. Another example of the two people in one that was Dulcy, he told himself as he rode past a line of serviceberry, halted, then moved into the trees where he began to watch her place. He had waited a little over an hour when he saw the lone rider leave and turn east. Fargo let him distance himself before he followed, watched the man go through town, and ride past the window of the saloon where the bartender no doubt saw him pass. Fargo smiled grimly, but turned the Ovaro away and rode back toward the canyon. He had other things to do before he put his own plans into action.

Dusk came down on the land as he entered the canyon, and he rode carefully as he neared the castle, melting into a cluster of red oak as he saw four of Averson's men riding back to the castle. He waited, let darkness fall, and watched the drawbridge raised and put into place. He edged the pinto out of the trees to the edge of the moat, dismounted, and shed clothes. Silently, he slid into the water of the moat and let himself go under the surface. Surprisingly, he found the water was not more than eight or nine feet deep as he swam underwater, passed the drawbridge, and surfaced a dozen yards beyond. He halted against the rocks of the castle wall, moonlight illuminating the slightly curved surface of the outer wall. It was too smooth to climb, he saw, but his eyes lingered at the edge of the drawbridge, where it rested upright into the opening of the wall.

It was a poor fit. A man could climb up it. His glance went to the embrasure only a few feet from the edge of the drawbridge, the vertical opening cut into a low portion of the wall. Thoughts turned in his mind as he surveyed the wall again, and then he sank underwater again and swam back to where he'd entered the moat. He pulled himself onto the land, took a towel from his saddlebag, and dried himself and pulled on clothes. Walking the Ovaro by the cheekstrap, he moved away from the moat before climbing onto the horse. He rode to the red oak, bedded down, slept, and woke with the new sun. He stayed in the trees, the castle clearly in sight, and watched the drawbridge lowered. A half dozen of Averson's men came out, patrolled along the front of the castle, and returned inside, leaving two as guards by the gate.

It was perhaps an hour later when Averson emerged on his horse, six of his men with him. They rode from the castle at a fast canter, heading east along the canyon, and he was about to leave the trees to follow them when four more of Averson's men rode from the castle. Fargo pulled the pinto back into the oak and waited, then saw the four men ride some hundred yards on and halt. They separated to form a picket line, rifles resting on their hips. Fargo swore silently. They'd see him if he left the oaks. He decided to stay and not to try to run their gauntlet. He estimated it was some three hours later when Roy Averson and the other six hands returned. The four riders standing guard followed the others back into the castle, and Fargo edged himself out of the oaks at the rear of the cluster.

A frown furrowed his brow as he rode along the far side of the canyon, scanning each of the farms and ranches as he passed. Everything appeared quiet and in order, and he finally turned at the Crew place, exchanged waves and returned to the red oak as dusk crept over the canyon. He bedded down, ate some cold beef jerky strips out of his saddlebag, and undressed and stretched out on his bedroll as the moon rose. Averson and his men had perhaps gone to town, he mused as he decided enough time had passed for the man to face reality. Maybe he'd confront him come morning and try again to reason with him, or perhaps he'd be able to give Roy Averson another dose of reality. Fargo went over possibilities before pulling sleep to himself to wake when the moon was at the far end of the sky, starting to dip down to the end of night.

He dressed, rode through the still, deep hours of the canyon, circled to the rear of the castle, and left the pinto in a thicket of bur oak. Moving quickly on foot, lariat in hand, he sent the rope whirling across the moat to catch around a low, gnarled tree that grew bare-branched alongside the wall. Fastening the other end of the lariat around a long oak where he stood, he secured the line that now stretched across the moat. Curling his legs around the rope, he pushed himself along the lariat, hand over hand across the moat, until he reached the other side. Dropping down to the strip of land that edged the castle, he stepped to the wall, where he had seen the uneven stones of the rear wall, and began to climb. Moving slowly, often with only a bare fingerhold to cling to, he worked his way up the wall, pausing flylike against the stones, to rest fingers, hands, and shoulder muscles. But finally he reached one of the embrasures and carefully peered through the narrow, vertical slit in the wall.

Seeing no one inside, he squeezed himself in and dropped to the stone floor as the first rays of dawn began to tint the sky. He drew the Colt and, moving on silent steps, made his way along the interior of the castle, where the passages were dimly lighted by kerosene lamps. He smiled. Averson had replaced the medieval authenticity of wall torches for the convenience of the lamps. Moving down a curved slight incline of stone steps, he made his way to Amy's room, going by where he mentally placed it from seeing her at the window. He reached the floor below and found himself silently cursing as he saw he'd been accurate. Six guards lounged in the passageway outside the thick, wooden door of Amy's room. He grimaced in another silent curse.

Even if he could take all six of them, he'd never get out with Amy. The gunfire would bring all the rest of Averson's men running. He backed silently along the passageway, moving away from the room, found another stone corridor, and went down it as the new day began to seep into the interior of the castle. He spotted a mock figure in a suit of armor standing in a corner of the corridor and saw the passageway widen beyond it with three closed doors at the other end. Sliding behind the armor-clad form, he scrunched down to hide himself, yet stayed upright enough to let him see out into the corridor beyond and the inner dimensions of a large room below.

The new day quickly filled the interior of the castle, and he heard sounds from below, then saw two men carrying a bucket of water across the large room, probably to the kitchen, he guessed. Others appeared, moved across the room, and went outside, and then Fargo heard the sound of one of the doors opening at the end of the corridor. His eyes narrowed on the door, and he saw Roy Averson come from the room, pulling on his shirt and without his gunbelt. The man walked toward the stairs at the other end of the corridor, and when he passed the suit of armor, Fargo stepped out, the Colt in his hand. "Surprise, surprise," he said softly.

Roy Averson's face blanched as he stared at Fargo, and his lips worked soundlessly for a moment before his voice finally followed. "You son of a bitch," he said, but beneath his fury he was still thoroughly shaken, Fargo knew. "Son of a bitch," Roy Averson repeated.

"Flattery will get you nowhere," Fargo said. "I've come for Amy."

8

"You're a crazy man, Fargo," Roy Averson breathed. "Fucking crazy."

"Maybe, but I want Amy," Fargo said.

"Go to hell."

"Give it up, Averson. You've no hold on anybody anymore. It's over for you. I'm giving you a chance to be reasonable. Give me Amy, and I'll work out something between you and Dulcy."

"Who're you kidding? That little bitch won't work out anything," the man said. "And nothin's over. Those stupid bastards are going to wish they'd never listened to you. I'll make them sorry for that, real sorry. You wait and see."

Fargo felt a stab of uneasiness at Roy Averson's intransigence. Was his bluster all hollow, simply a sign that he still refused to face reality? Or did he still have some plan to strike back? "Give me Amy," Fargo said. "Leave her out of the rest of this."

"Go screw yourself," the man snarled.

"My trigger finger's getting awfully itchy," Fargo said.

"Go ahead. You won't get Amy, and you'll never get out alive," Roy Averson said defiantly.

Fargo swore to himself. Whether out of self-delusion or stubborn desperation, Averson refused to budge, and

Fargo realized there was no way he could shoot his way out with Amy. It would take another way to get her, another time, another place, another opportunity. Perhaps Amy herself could provide that, he reflected, but he'd need time to think more about that. Now he had to get himself out of the castle alive, so he pushed the Colt into Roy Averson's ribs. "We're going outside together," he said. "One wrong move, and it's really over for you. You don't want that, do you?" Averson's silence showed that Fargo had reached the man. Roy Averson was desperate enough to pay the ultimate price if he had to, but smart enough to avoid that if he could. "Walk," Fargo growled, and, staying close to the man, he began to go down the curved stone steps.

He held Averson's arm with one hand while pressing the gun barrel into his ribs with the other as he walked tight against the man. Two of Averson's men halted at their chores to stare, frowns of uncertainty wrinkling their brows. One man's hand started toward his gun, and Fargo pushed the Colt harder into Averson's ribs. "It's all right. Stay back," Averson called out, and the men froze in place. The same thing happened as Fargo walked into the outside courtyard with him and Averson called out again.

"Very good. That's being real smart," Fargo said to the man as they crossed the drawbridge, the rifle-carrying guards looking on. Reaching the end of the drawbridge, Fargo moved toward the thicket of bur oak where he had left the Ovaro. Glancing back, he saw six of Averson's men following, the two sentries with their rifles and four others. "Tell them to stay back," Fargo ordered, and Averson called out again. The men slowed, but didn't stop, and Fargo reached the trees, stepped away from Averson, and swung onto the pinto. "Get smart. Come to your senses. No more playing the lord. The games are over. Bring Amy and nobody gets hurt," Fargo said in a last try at reaching Roy Averson.

"Screw you," the man hissed, and Fargo turned the horse and started through the trees. He immediately flung himself low across the jet-black neck and put the pinto into a gallop as Averson's voice screamed orders. "Shoot, goddammit. Kill the bastard."

The hail of bullets whistled through the trees, thudded into thick tree trunks, and snapped off thin branches. But they were all wild, and Fargo left the frustrated fusillade behind as he raced away. Once beyond the trees at the other side, he slowed to an easy trot and straightened up in the saddle. He'd come away empty-handed, but it had not been a total failure. His appearance inside the castle had shaken Averson, made him aware that he was far from invincible even inside his medieval domain. His reaction was predictable. He'd drape the castle with guards, inside and outside, for a while, at least. It'd keep most of his men tied up. If he had any plans to hit back at the ranchers, he'd have to put them on hold.

But there'd be no chance to get to Amy inside the castle now, Fargo realized. Yet perhaps Amy held the key to her own rescue. She'd not stay cooped up in the castle. Not headstrong, willful, demanding little Amy. Averson would have to let her ride her pony outside. He'd surround her with guards, yet he'd have to do it. Staying on Amy's good side was all-important to him, and Fargo's eyes narrowed in thought. He'd have to plan a way to take Amy when those moments came. Perhaps he'd need help, he pondered. He had done the people of the canyon a service they'd never hoped to find. Perhaps it was time to call on them to return the favor. They'd do it, he felt certain. They were good people and grateful. He'd make plans, talk to them, and then wait for the right moment, he decided.

He neared the Crew place, and turned toward it, a frown at his brow as he saw the small knot of people with Loretta standing by. He recognized Jed Offerman as he drew closer, and two other men he knew only by sight. They turned to him as he rode up, and saw the concern on their faces. "We were going to come searching for you," Jed Offerman said.

"What's going on. You've trouble in your faces," Fargo said.

"Big trouble," Jed Offerman said. "We just came from the bank. My cousin, Thomas, died back in Kansas. Thomas was always well off, and I just got a letter with a check. He left me enough money to pay off my note at the bank, so I decided I'd do that first thing. Seth and Ezra here went along with me, and we met with Ben Hopkins. I told him what I wanted to do, and he said he'd pass that on."

"Pass that on?" Fargo frowned. "What's that mean?"

"Just what I asked," Jed Offerman said. "He told me it meant my note had been sold."

"He said all our notes were sold," the man named Ezra put in. "Ben Hopkins said it's done all the time. He said notes are like any other asset the bank has—properties, mortgages, contracts, whatever. They can sell them off anytime they want to raise money."

"Our notes were a bloc they could sell off as one deal, he said," Offerman added.

"Who'd he sell them to?" Fargo questioned.

"He said that was confidential information," Offerman said. "But we know who bought our notes, don't we? Roy Averson, that's who. It's all too damn pat. Who else would show up suddenly and buy all our notes?"

Fargo scanned their faces filled with despair and fear and felt the sinking feeling in the pit of his own stomach. It fit, he muttered silently. It explained Roy Averson's unbending attitude, his belligerence, his very words. The threats he had flung suddenly took on new meaning, no longer hollow bluster.

"You know what this means, Fargo," Harry Crew said. "He owns us again, more than he ever did before. We're worse off than we ever were. Now he'll take his revenge. We'll all be paying as we never paid before."

Fargo wanted to offer words of hope and courage, but realized he had none to give. "You just sit tight. I'm going to see about this. Maybe I can do something. Don't get down yet," he said and knew that the advice sounded hollow. "I'll be back tonight. Have everyone meet me here. There's no need to bring the womenfolk," he said and saw Loretta blow him a kiss as he rode away at a fast canter. He refused to let helplessness sweep over him, but he couldn't stop the churning anger that stayed inside him. He kept the Ovaro at the fast canter all the way to Big Dusty, where he reined to a halt before the bank. He strode into the building and saw Ben Hopkins talking to an elderly man in a green eyeshade behind the teller's cage.

"Fargo," the banker said in surprise. "What brings you here?"

"I want some answers, about notes," Fargo said, his voice hard.

"Leave us alone, Harold," Hopkins said to the clerk, who went to an adjoining room and pulled the door closed after him.

"I heard you sold off those notes," Fargo said to the banker. "Awfully sudden, wasn't it?"

"I got a good offer. It made good business sense. A simple transaction," Hopkins said.

"Who'd you sell them to?" Fargo questioned.

"I'm afraid that's confidential," the banker said.

"Why?"

"It's the usual way. It's up to the buyer to notify the noteholders anytime he wishes to do so, usually when a payment comes due. Meanwhile, the bank continues to act as collection agent until the new noteholder notifies us otherwise or until a payment is overdue."

"What happens then?"

"We notify the new noteholder. Under the terms in the notes, the holder has the right to call in the entire amount if a payment is missed," Hopkins said.

"And it's pretty damn sure folks will miss a payment at some time or another," Fargo said.

"Yes, but not all noteholders exercise that right," the man said.

"This one will," Fargo said. "It's Roy Averson, isn't it? He worked a deal with you for the whole package."

"I told you, that's confidential. I can't comment on that."

"I can. It stinks. Make it unconfidential. I want to see the details for myself. Fact is, I want you to cancel the whole goddamn sale," Fargo said.

"Impossible," Ben Hopkins said stiffly.

"Maybe I can show you how to make it possible. Let me see the goddamn contract," Fargo said.

"That would be entirely out of order. I wouldn't do anything of the kind," the banker said adamantly.

"Tell me it wasn't Roy Averson," Fargo threw at him.

"I can't answer that," Hopkins said.

"You just did," Fargo snapped and stormed out of the bank. Dulcy was close enough for him to stop at her place first, and she listened to what he told her had happened, first at the castle and then at the bank. "You talk to Hopkins," Fargo said. "Get him to return Averson's purchase money and pull out of the deal."

"I haven't that kind of influence with him," she said. "He is a banker, after all. He made a transaction as a banker. He won't change that, not for me, not for anybody."

"Try," Fargo said.

"I don't have to. I know the man," Dulcy said. "And none of this concerns Amy. That's what you're supposed to be thinking about."

"It concerns her. I was going to call on the ranchers to help me get Amy. Now I can't count on their gratitude," he said.

"That's your problem. Solve it," Dulcy said icily.

"You're all sympathy today," Fargo said.

"Get Amy, and I'll be all sympathy," Dulcy snapped. He nodded, turned, and walked from the house as dusk began to settle. He rode away wrapped in grimness. Everything had collapsed around him, all the good things he'd tried to do swept away, his plans for taking Amy shattered. But one answer took shape in his thoughts as he rode into the canyon. He let that answer find details, pull itself from a thought into a plan, and when he reached the Crew place, it had become concrete. He saw the knot of men waiting and rode to a halt and dismounted, his eyes sweeping the group and pausing on Bill Ulrich and his sons. They had suddenly become the keys to his plan.

"I couldn't get what I wanted out of Ben Hopkins," he told them candidly. "But I have to go along with you. Averson bought all your notes from the bank."

"And he owns us again," someone said. "We're back in

the same boat, only worse. Now he has the deeds to all our lands."

"You've only one choice left," Fargo said. "Fight. Get yourselves together and go after him before he picks you apart one by one."

"We can't win. We can't attack him behind his goddamn castle. He'll slaughter us," Ben Bentley said. "We'd need cannon to break through. The nearest army post with any artillery is probably Fort Dodge way down in Missouri territory, and they don't lend out cannon, and they don't take part in private fights."

"But there is a way to attack his castle, the same way castles were attacked in the Middle Ages. He's been playing the role of a medieval lord. Now you can give it back to him with medieval weapons. There'll be a wonderful irony to it, though I don't think he'll appreciate it," Fargo said.

"What medieval weapons?" someone asked.

"The ones you'll build from the pictures I'll draw for you," Fargo said and turned to Bill Ulrich. "You told me you can build anything. I'll give you drawings you can work from. You'll build inside those four big barns so any of Averson's boys come past they won't see anything."

"I've got my forge, my bellows, all my tools. I can do it, but I'd need a lot more help to do it fast," Ulrich said.

"Everybody will work under you, men, women, and children," Fargo said. "You build the weapons, and I'll lead the attack."

"We've nothing to lose," Jed Offerman said. "Hell, I'd rather fight than live under Roy Averson's thumb again. Start drawing, Fargo."

"Come inside. I've a pad and pencil," Loretta said, and the others talked among themselves as Fargo followed her into the house. He was seated at the table with one drawing almost finished when they all came inside. He'd pulled on his memory of the book he had once read and was glad he had spent so much time studying it. He showed his first drawing to the others as they crowded around.

"This is called a mangonel," he said and pointed to the device that employed a long, spoon-shaped arm on which a heavy stone was placed. The arm was made tight by heavy rope cables, and when it was released, it threw the heavy stone with tremendous force, the force of a cannon, that could knock a hole in a castle wall. Next he drew a picture of a belfry, a tall wooden assault tower some twenty feet high with a roof and six thick, wooden wheels. Ladders and platforms inside held up to twenty men. Wheeled up against the very walls of the castle, it let the attackers climb from the belfry over the tops of the lower walls. The last device he drew was a structure braced by wooden supports that lay flat on the ground.

"They call this a trebuchet," he said. "The long wooden arm has a huge leather pouch at one end, and it works on the principle of a giant slingshot. The throwing arm is held down at one end by ropes and a windlass. Stones are loaded into the sling, and when the arm is released, it fires the sling. The stones hit and scatter like shrapnel."

Ulrich and his sons studied the drawings. "We can do it. While the men are building, the women and kids can bring in heavy stones for the mangonel and the smaller ones for this trebuchet slingshot affair."

"Have them collect bundles of branches, about twenty-five bundles," Fargo said.

"What are they for?"

"To put into the moat to form a bridge for the belfry so it can be rolled into the moat and pushed against the castle wall," Fargo said. "When we're ready, we move by night, get there just at dawn. We'll use your plowhorses to pull the weapons into place. Meanwhile, keep a sentry patrol around your barns, Bill."

"You think Averson will be coming by?" Ulrich asked.

"One of his boys might. Right now, he's waiting a spell. I've got him keeping most of his men at the castle. I got inside once, and he wants to be sure I don't do it again. How long do you figure it'll take you to finish?"

"We work day and night, I'd say about a week. They won't be the quality of the old medieval pieces, I'm sure, but they'll work, well enough for what we have to do."

"Good. Averson's castle is only a pale copy of the real ones. Get all your people together and get started tonight. Every minute counts. I'll be a while before I stop by to check things," Fargo said.

"You sound like you're going away," Harry Crew said.

"For a day or two," Fargo said.

"All right, you heard the man," Bill Ulrich called out. "Let's get to my place and start getting my equipment in place." Fargo stayed as the men hurried from the house, then he felt Loretta's shoulder against his.

"Where are you going?" she asked.

"To take out an insurance policy, you might say," he answered.

"That doesn't tell me much," she sniffed.

"It's better that way," he said.

"You still going to follow Dulcy Washburn's orders?" she asked. "Things have changed now."

"Not enough yet," he said as she walked to the pinto with him and clung to him with the edge of a pout on her lips before he climbed onto the horse. He rode away wondering whether becoming a woman always meant becoming possessive.

The moon had climbed high into the night sky when he reached Dulcy's place and found her still up, her opaque blue eyes searching his face behind their pale-fire mask.

"Make any big decisions?" she asked.

"There's no way to get to Averson except the hard way, an all-out attack," he said.

"What about Amy?" Dulcy asked.

"I'll go get Amy while the others fight," he said.

"And what if you don't get to her?"

He shrugged. "I expect to get her."

"It's not enough. I want to be in on it," she said.

"I can't take care of you and get Amy," he said.

"I'll take care of myself. You failed twice to get to Amy. I want to be there this time. Let me know when you're going to move against him," Dulcy said. "That's an order."

"Seems to me you're giving an awful lot of orders that aren't part of the deal, honey," he said.

"They're all part of the deal until you get Amy," she said, and he decided not to answer, turned, and walked from the house. She didn't call after him, he noted, and realized he wasn't at all bothered by that. Dulcy had become too much of an enigma for him. He rode into the night and bedded down a few thousand yards from her place, slept till morning came, and slowly dressed. He stayed in the trees where he could see to the gatepost to Dulcy's place, relaxed, and let the morning pass. The sun had crossed into the early afternoon when he saw the lone rider pass through the gatepost and head south.

He climbed into the saddle and stayed back as he followed the man's trail, half smiled as the hoofprints led through town, past the saloon window, and went on. He continued to follow, the pace leisurely, then saw the hoofprints turn west and go into a long hollow bordered by wild geranium and tanbark oak. The afternoon began to draw to a close, and the trail continued along the long, narrow hollow, the lone set of prints easy to see. The narrow stretch of lush land stretched on when a sudden growth of oak grew across the hollow to form a leafy wall. Fargo slid from the saddle and led the Ovaro through the green barrier, pushed his way slowly, hardly disturbing a leaf. He reached the end of the trees and halted, then peered out to where the narrow hollow continued on again. A small cabin rested to one side of the long hollow, and Fargo saw the horse tethered outside.

He turned and made his way deeper into the trees to where they met the right side of the hollow and another heavy growth of tanbark oak. Tethering the horse to a low branch, he went forward on careful steps that brought him to the rear of the cabin. He saw three more horses there, two unsaddled. Aware that the afternoon was turning to dusk, he crept closer to the cabin and saw a window at each side and a stone chimney rising up to the sloping roof at the rear. Fargo waited, let the dusk become dark, and saw a lamp turned on inside the cabin, its yellow finger of light reaching out from the nearest window. As he stood motionless, the rider he had followed came from the cabin door, swung onto his horse, and rode away. Fargo heard him pushing his way through the trees that formed the wall across the hollow. He'd delivered his message and was on his way back to Dulcy.

Fargo let the night deepen before he crept to the window and carefully peered inside. Paula sat on a narrow cot against one wall of the cabin. She looked depressed, but he saw no marks on her, and she showed no signs of not being fed. Three men were reclining on the floor at the other side of the room, and Fargo saw a rope that had been strung across the ceiling where a curtain hung at one end to separate the room. Paula moved, shifting her position on the cot, and he saw the rope around one ankle, followed it with his eyes, and saw that it was long enough to give her some freedom of movement. He found the other end and saw it was nailed down to the floor, the nails bent over to securely fasten the rope to the floorboards. The front door of the cabin was ajar, he saw, and moving on steps silent as a panther's, he crept to the other side of the door. He picked up a length of broken branch and scraped it along the back of the door. "That damn 'possum again," somebody said from inside.

"Go put a bullet in the critter. He kept us awake all night last night," another voice said. Fargo pressed himself in the blackness against the back of the partly open door, the butt of the Colt raised in one hand. The man stepped from the door, slipping through without opening it further, and paused outside to peer into the darkness. Fargo moved the branch against the door again. The man whirled, then came around the back of the door as he drew his gun. Fargo crashed the Colt down onto his head and caught him before he hit the ground. Lifting the man, he carried the unconscious figure behind the cabin, deposited him silently on the ground, and returned to the cabin. Dropping to one knee, he pressed himself against the cabin only inches from the door, holding the Colt by the grip this time.

He waited, hardly breathing. "Charlie, you out there?" a voice called from inside the cabin after a few minutes. Fargo let the silence answer. "Go see what happened to Charlie," the voice ordered, and Fargo heard a figure move toward the door. The man came out, short, baldheaded, and Fargo leaped to his feet. Surprise flooded the man's face as he saw Fargo. "Back inside," Fargo said, the Colt aimed at the man's chest. The man backed into the cabin, and Fargo saw the third man look up, his jaw dropping. "Don't do anything dumb, or your friend here gets it," Fargo said. The man half rose as Fargo heard Paula's yelp of recognition and delight. She rose from the cot and started toward him. Fargo saw the third man dive for her. He shifted the Colt, fired, and the figure dropped almost at Paula's feet. The bald-headed man in front of him made the mistake of thinking he had time to draw his gun. He managed to clear the holster and bring it half up when a shot sent him flying backward in a shower of scarlet.

Fargo lowered the Colt as Paula flung her arms around him. "Oh, God, are you ever a sight for sore eyes," she cried out.

He saw a kitchen knife on the floor near the fireplace and used it to cut the rope from around her ankle. "You all right?" he asked her as she clung to him.

"I guess so," she said. "They didn't touch me, if that's what you mean. A lot of threats, but nothing else. They kept telling me you were dead, but I didn't believe them."

"I'm going to take you home," Fargo said. "There's a horse you can ride around back."

"What happened to that bitch that had them take me here? She was made of ice," Paula said and gave a little shiver.

"Ice and fire," Fargo corrected. "She's very much around. She made a pawn out of you for much bigger things she wants."

"Where is she now?" Paula asked as she threw her few things into a sack.

"Waiting for me," Fargo said, and she frowned. "A long story. I'll tell you on the way," he said and started out of the cabin with her. They had just gone outside when a shot sent splinters from the edge of the door.

Fargo dived to the ground, pulling Paula with him, then rolled with her as another two shots slammed into the dirt. Charlie had come around faster than expected, Fargo swore as he rolled again, came up against a low mountain laurel bush, and drew the Colt. He saw the flash as Charlie fired again and heard the bullet hurtle through the bush. He fired at the spot where he'd seen the flash, four shots only inches apart. He heard the man's gargled cry of pain, followed by another, and then there was silence. Fargo waited, Paula crushed against him, reached out, and let his fingers pick up a handful of small stones. He flung them to one side, but there was no answering shot, so he pushed to his feet with Paula. "I didn't hit him hard enough," he muttered. "Let's go."

Riding one of the horses behind the cabin, Paula listened as Fargo told her everything that had happened. The morning sun came up before he finished, and they paused at a pond to let everyone drink. "Doesn't seem to me you have to go back," Paula said. "They sound like they deserve each other. Like father like daughter. It's in the blood."

"I've thought that, but I keep hoping there is a difference. Right now Daddy has the edge on rottenness. Then there's little Amy. But I'm really going back to help the people in the canyon finish on top," Fargo said, and Paula rode in silence beside him as they continued on.

The midday sun burned down when they reached her place, and she breathed a long sigh. "Didn't know if I'd ever see this place again," she said. "Can you stay?"

"I'd best start back," he said, and Paula finally took her arms from around him.

"I'll be here, whenever you want," she said. "But I don't have to tell you that, do I?"

"No," he replied as he put the Ovaro into a trot.

9

He didn't hurry, partly because tiredness pulled hard at him. Finding a small hollow in a stand of staghorn sumac as the sun went down, he set out his bedroll and slept soundly through the night. In the morning he held to his leisurely pace and reached the canyon just before dark and rode immediately to the Ulrich place. He was surprised at how much work had been done, the mangonel and the trebuchet both finished, the belfry almost done. They were crudely fashioned, he saw, but they'd do for one all-out attack. Bill Ulrich showed him the large stones and the smaller rocks inside a sturdy two-horse farm wagon, along with the bundles of brush.

"Any visitors come looking?" he asked.

"Just two of Averson's men, but they rode by," Ulrich said.

"Good. That means he's still waiting for me to come calling," Fargo said. "Bring the plowhorses in after dark tomorrow, as many as you have. We'll need every one of them."

"We built wheeled platforms to move the trebuchet and the mangonel. We'll be ready to go in two nights," Bill Ulrich said.

"I'll be here," Fargo said and went on through the night that had settled over the canyon. Dulcy still had the extra guards in place when he arrived, he noted, and she was standing in the living room when he entered. The pale blue-fire eyes were narrowed as they fastened on him.

"I wondered if you'd even come back," she said, her voice tight.

"Guess you found out," he said.

"Of course I found out. My next day's messenger came racing back to tell me. You feeling real pleased with yourself?" she tossed at him.

"No. I should've done it a lot sooner," Fargo said.

"Didn't you think I'd keep our deal?" she asked, accusation in her voice.

"You're two people. I'm never sure which one I'll see," he said. "I decided I couldn't take any chances."

"Why did you come back then?" she pressed.

"For Amy. I'd like to see her out of his hands. And for the people in the canyon."

"I'll settle for that. You don't have to like me. Just get Amy," she said. "And I'm still going to be there."

"Your call," he said, turned, and started for the door. He had just reached it when she called to him. "You'll like me again when it's all over. I'll see to that," she said. A deep sigh came from his lips as he walked outside. She was still the enigma, a beautiful, infuriating puzzle. And that first night with her still simmered in his mind. He pushed aside all thoughts of Dulcy as he rode away. He had more important plans to put into final shape.

He went over those plans on his bedroll beside a stream until he fell asleep, then went over them again when he woke after he washed and dressed by the stream. When he finally rode to the Ulrich place, he arranged for everyone to meet early the next night. The rest of the day was spent preparing the special harnesses needed for the horses to pull the wheeled platforms and the belfry, and when night fell, he bedded down at the outskirts of the Ulrich sheds and was ready to go to work again with the new day. It was when the day began to draw to an end that he spoke to the others about Dulcy. "She insists on taking part in it," he said. "I figure we can use every hand we can get."

"Doesn't bother us any," Jed Offerman said. "Guess any fight against Roy Averson is her fight, too."

"It is," Fargo said, glad for the acceptance they'd given. It made him feel more comfortable when, after night fell, and everyone gathered at the Ulrich place, Dulcy arrived, joining the other women where they waited. All except Loretta. He found her to one side beside her mother. Fargo waved everyone into a circle inside the main shed. "The sentries will see us when we reach the castle. We'll time it so's to get there just before dawn. They'll start firing at once," Fargo said. "In the dark they won't be very accurate. The first thing is to get the belfry smack up against the wall. The horses will pull it to the very edge of the moat. You women will have the job of throwing the bundles of branches into the moat so the belfry won't sink when we push it across."

"What do we do when we're finished?" someone asked.

"Take cover behind the belfry and start firing. You're all carrying rifles or six-guns. Dawn will be up by then," Fargo said and turned to the men. "Who's going to man the mangonel?" he asked, and a half dozen hands went up. "You fire first. Aim at the wall alongside the castle gate. Keep firing stones at the same spot. Soon as you've knocked a hole in the wall, you stop firing the mangonel and fight your way through the hole. When you're inside, lower the drawbridge. Now, who's going to be on the trebuchet?"

Four hands rose into the air, two of them women's. "While they're firing the mangonel, we keep firing the trebuchet," one of the women said. "Only we fire higher and send the rocks sailing over the top of the wall."

"Bull's-eye," Fargo said. "When the wall is breached, swing the arm on the trebuchet and keep firing, keep peppering the interior of the courtyard and the inner walls. Now hitch up the horses and let's move. It'll be a long, slow march."

He led the Ovaro to the front as the horses were hitched to the belfry and the wheeled platforms for the mangonel and the trebuchet and found Dulcy there. "I'll be inside the belfry with you," she said. "And over the wall behind you."

"I won't be looking to you," Fargo said. "You'll be on your own. I'll be going after Amy."

"I'll take care of myself," she said and returned to where the other women began to walk alongside the wagon that held the bundles of branches. He glimpsed the big Remington in the waistline of her skirt as he immersed himself in his own thoughts. He felt the tension gathering inside him with every step. It wasn't his alone, he was certain. Each and every one of the others were experiencing the same inner tightness. Their happiness, their futures, their lands, their very lives depended on the results of the impending battle. But they had one advantage they probably didn't realize. Everything they had depended on winning. They would fight with a fury and a desperation Averson's men could never summon. Hired hands had no reason to give their all. They hadn't the same stake in the outcome. It was the salient difference Fargo hoped would tip the balance.

The march was agonizingly slow, yet it hardly seemed slow at all as excitement seized everyone with each passing step until finally, through the deep of the predawn night, the walls and the turrets of the castle rose up before them. Fargo motioned as they moved closer to the dark bulk of stone that blotted out the moon, and the women came forward with the farm wagon. The six horses pulling the belfry moved forward in a straight line, only a dozen yards from the moat now, and Fargo heard the sudden shouts from atop the castle walls. Shots followed the shouts, only a few at first, then a volley, and Fargo moved alongside the belfry. The women were tossing the bundles of branches into the moat, atop each other in three sections.

"Cross," Fargo shouted, and the belfry rolled forward on its wide wooden wheels. The horses went into the moat, and Fargo shouted commands. "Unhitch them, quickly," he ordered, and as four men unhitched the horses, everyone else got behind the belfry and pushed. The horses were led away before they kicked aside the bundles of branches, and sixty shoulders pushed the belfry into the moat. It would surely have sunk to the bottom of the moat if it hadn't been for the bundles that served as a tenuous floor. But it rolled forward and came against the outer wall, and Fargo ran inside the structure, then climbed a ladder behind some of the men already pulling themselves to the top. Gunfire was heavy now, along with shouts, and he heard Roy Averson's voice above everything, shouting commands, yelling orders. He also heard the thumping crash of the first stone as it crashed into the wall, then the clatter of smaller rocks as the giant slingshot went into action. Cries of pain told him the rocks had found targets. He was moving behind Jed Offerman as he jumped from the belfry onto the top of the castle wall. Two figures came along the wall, rifles raised, and Fargo dropped low as he fired. Both figures screamed as they toppled over the wall.

Others were leaping from the belfry, firing, being met with counterfire from Averson's men from platforms behind the walls. Others fired from the embrasures in the near turret, but the attackers were running and firing like so many ants swarming in all directions. He heard another thudding crash and the shouts that followed as a piece of the wall gave way to leave a jagged hole. "Damn," he swore and dived to the ground, hands over his head as a shower of rocks crashed down into the inner court. Those at the trebuchet had quickly swung the arm around, and he rolled, feeling a rock graze his leg, another his foot.

The battle was raging, and he cast a quick glance around, searching for Dulcy's dark blond hair, but didn't see her. He got to his feet, but stayed in a crouch as he ran toward the front of the castle and Amy's room. A shot sent stone chips over him, and he dived as the next shot skinned his leg. He hit the ground on his back, the Colt raised, and saw the man aiming again with a rifle. He fired, and the man staggered, the rifle falling from his hands before he collapsed. Fargo rolled to his feet, saw the opening to the stone steps, and raced inside. He paused at an opening in the corridor wall and glanced out to see that the dawn had come up.

Below, in the courtyard, knots of figures exchanged gunfire, and some fought hand-to-hand while others ran, stopped behind stone columns to fire, and then ran again. It could have been a scene from a battle in the Middle Ages, except for the rifles and six-guns instead of swords and battle-axes. He looked for Averson, but didn't find him. Dulcy had disappeared also, and he went on down the corridor, turned a corner, and saw Amy's room, the door closed. He reached it, saw it was bolted from the outside, pulled the bolt back, and pushed the door open. Amy stared back at him, fully dressed, her round face expressionless. "Roy said I'd be safest here," she told him.

"He was wrong. Let's go," Fargo said.

"Where?" Amy asked, not moving.

"Out of here and back to your mother," Fargo said. "I hope," he added. Amy still didn't move, and behind him he heard a cheer and then Bill Ulrich's voice.

"That's it, run, you stinkin' cowards," Ulrich cried. Fargo felt satisfaction sweep through him. The drawbridge had been lowered, and at least some of Averson's men were fleeing across it. He returned his attention to Amy.

"Let's go," he said to the child. "You're going with me."

"No, she isn't," Averson's voice said, and Fargo felt the gun barrel pressed into his back. "I'll take that," Averson said and pulled the Colt from Fargo's hand. He stepped back and Fargo turned to face him. "The minute I saw the goddamn belfry I knew it was you," Roy Averson said. "And I knew this was where you'd come. I came here and waited down the corridor. Now we're all going to walk out. Anyone shoots at us, they could kill Amy, and none of us wants that. Besides, anyone shoots and I kill you, and you don't want that, either."

"You won't get away with it, even if we get out of here," Fargo said.

"Move," Averson rasped, and Fargo swore silently. He had to buy time, wait for a chance to strike back. That meant going along with Averson's orders, but he kept his grip on Amy's arm as they left the room. They walked into the corridor, and the gunfire had almost stopped as they went down the stone steps. Averson held the Colt pushed into his ribs, but Fargo kept his grip on Amy. When they reached the courtyard, he saw at least eight of Averson's men lying lifeless on the stone floor. Harry Crew and three others were on the ground, bandaging their wounded, and he saw the Ulrichs rise to their feet as he moved across the yard with Averson and the child. They frowned, rifles half raised, uncertainty in their faces.

"No . . . don't shoot," Fargo said as others came forward. None of them were marksmen. They'd fire in a volley, and that could be disastrous, he knew. He kept walking, Averson at his side, Amy halfway in front of him.

"Keep walking," the man growled, and Fargo saw the drawbridge in front of them. Amy made no move to escape from his grip, and her contained silence was both astonishing and unsettling. They crossed the drawbridge, and Fargo saw Jed Offerman, a bandage around his head, come forward with two other men, helplessness in their faces. He glimpsed Loretta standing with three other women, fear in her face as he moved over the drawbridge. But they all had the sense to stay back, and he was grateful for that. He spotted the Ovaro standing among the other horses a few dozen yards from the end of the drawbridge. Averson pushed him to one of the horses, stepped back a pace, but kept the gun leveled at him. "Let go of her," he ordered. Fargo was about to refuse when Amy tore from his grip. "Good girl," Averson said and gestured to the horse. "Get on."

Amy pulled herself onto the horse, and Fargo let his knees bend as he tightened every muscle in his legs, certain of Averson's next move. Turning his body as he leaped, he flung himself into a twisting dive a split second before the shot rang out. He felt the bullet graze his back as he hit the ground rolling, kept rolling, aware that his instant of anticipation had saved his life. When he had a second to glance up, he saw Roy Averson racing away on the horse with Amy, fleeing before anyone else could come up. He pulled himself to his feet, ran for the Ovaro, and vaulted into the saddle. As he wheeled the horse to give chase, Jed Offerman tossed him a six-gun as he went by, and Fargo put the Ovaro into a gallop. He closed distance quickly, and Averson heard him coming, made a sharp right turn, then fled alongside a line of hackberry with a stream paralleling the trees.

Fargo rode into the trees, spurred the Ovaro on and, still inside the hackberry, passed Averson with Amy sitting in the saddle in front of him. When he had enough distance, he veered sharply out of the trees and reined to a halt, blocking Averson's path. Averson reined to a halt, his eyes on the gun Fargo held leveled at him. "You going to shoot through her?" he asked as he held Amy to him.

"No. You know that," Fargo said, and Averson sneered. Fargo swung from the saddle, but kept the revolver trained on Averson. He decided to try to reach Averson by shaming him in front of Amy. "Your grandpa's using you as a shield. That shows you how much he cares about you, Amy," he said. Amy turned her head to look up at Averson.

"Don't listen to him," Averson growled.

"Are you?" Amy asked.

"No, goddammit," Averson roared.

"Let me get down," Amy said with icy calm.

Averson's mouth twisted as his face filled with fury. "Get down," he bit out, and Amy slid from the horse. "Goddamn you, Fargo," Averson snarled as, keeping the Colt trained, he swung from the saddle. "Stand over there, baby," he said to Amy, who moved to the side, her back to the stream. Averson faced Fargo, both men with their guns aimed directly at each other. "Go on, Mister Big. Shoot and we're both dead," he said.

Fargo swore silently. Averson was all too right. At this range there'd be no winner, and Fargo's mind raced. He was reluctant to pay the ultimate price, he realized. Amy was only one part of it. He hadn't seen Dulcy since the attack started. Maybe she'd gone down. Self-sacrifice would be but a hollow gesture then. And he couldn't let it all revolve around Amy. There was more at stake, perhaps enough to make Averson see reason. "We can deal," he said. "Amy's not all of it. Give me the notes, and I'll back off."

Averson frowned. "Notes? What notes?"

"The ones you bought back from the bank," Fargo said.

Averson's frown deepened. "I didn't buy any notes back from Ben Hopkins," he said and suddenly erupted in a harsh, bitter laugh. "Jesus, I told you you weren't smart enough to see all of it. But she was. Jesus, yes. She bought the goddamn notes. The little bitch took in all of you."

"Dulcy?" Fargo frowned.

"Of course, Dulcy. Your idea was to pay me off with bank notes, only she saw the possibilities in it. That's why she went along with you, probably promised her ass to Ben Hopkins. I told you Dulcy never does anyone any favors. Everything is hers now. Christ, you're all fools."

Fargo stared back, the man's words throbbing inside him. All lies or all brutal truth, he wondered. The question hung in front of him, vibrating with an evil aura of its own. He was still wrestling with all it meant when he heard a sound behind him, then half turned to see Dulcy, the big Remington in her hand.

"I saw you in the castle, saw you leave with him. I followed and circled around the other way. I've been waiting for you to shoot him. Are you going to do it or not?" she asked.

"I'm not much for suicide," Fargo said and met Dulcy's opaque blue eyes. "Is it true about the notes?" he asked. "Did you buy them from Ben Hopkins?"

"That doesn't concern you," she snapped, and Fargo tasted the bitterness in his mouth and knew he'd had his answer.

"Goddamn," he breathed softly. "Paula was right. There is no difference."

Dulcy's pale-fire blue eyes dismissed him with an expressionless glance as she stared at Roy Averson. "You can't get us both, so put the gun down," she said to him.

"And have you shoot me down, you little bitch," Averson said. Dulcy's eyes stayed expressionless, Fargo saw.

"You're not getting Amy," she said.

"You sure as hell aren't," Averson flung back.

With a sense of horror Fargo saw Dulcy's finger start to tighten on the trigger. A quick glance showed Roy Averson's trigger finger pulling back. Fargo hadn't even time to shout. He was between them, and he had time only to throw himself backward as the two shots rang out almost as one. He hit the ground on his back, managed to look up, and saw Roy Averson and Dulcy sink to the ground, twin stains of red spreading over both their chests. "Jesus," he said as he pushed to his feet, and his eyes went to Amy where she stood against the edge of the stream. She was motionless, not a sound from her, only her eyes moving from one prone figure to the other.

"Stupid," she said finally. "Really stupid." She turned to Fargo, and he stared at her totally contained calmness, her face mirroring faint disdain.

"I'll take you back," he said.

"I'll get my things. Then you can take me to Ben Hopkins," she said.

"Why Ben Hopkins?" Fargo asked as he helped her onto the Ovaro and climbed on behind her.

"Aunt Clara made arrangements in case anything happened to Dulcy and Roy. She was a very smart woman," Amy said as Fargo paused to retrieve his Colt. "There's a man and his wife in Massachusetts who've been paid to stand by to take care of me. Ben Hopkins has all the papers and the bank holds the funds. He'll handle everything for me to go there."

"That's good," Fargo said and realized he felt at a loss for words in front of Amy's calm, cool matter-of-factness. Amy stayed silent as they rode, and they were approaching the castle when Fargo spoke again. "There are some bank notes your mother has. As her heir, they'll be yours. It'd be good if you return them to the bank. I can get Ben Hopkins to buy them back from you."

"Notes from the ranchers and farmers," Amy said, and he nodded. "Notes with all their lands as . . . what's the word?"

"Collateral," Fargo said. "That's why it'd be best if the bank held their notes. They're all good people. They've been through enough."

"Dulcy used to talk about their lands being very valuable," Amy said.

"Probably, but it'd be right if you turned the notes back to the bank," he said.

Amy's little face was expressionless, but he saw her eyes narrow in thought. "I don't think so," she said finally and very quietly.

"What?" Fargo frowned at her as they entered the castle.

"In six years I'll be on my own. I'll be able to do whatever I want with the money Aunt Clara left me and with anything else. That means those notes."

"What'll you do with them?"

Amy gave a little smile. "I've seen those people. They'll fall behind in their payments. You can count on it. I'll have a lot of very valuable land. Six years isn't a long time to wait," she said, then dropped down from the horse and hurried off to get her things. Fargo stopped staring after her only when the others crowded around him.

"We did it," Jed Offerman said. "We won. We've some wounded, but nothing we can't treat."

"What happened to Roy Averson?" someone called.

"Dead. Dulcy, too," Fargo said.

"My God," a woman gasped.

"What about our notes? Can we get them?" Bill Ulrich asked.

"He never had them. It was Dulcy," Fargo said and heard the murmur of shock. "They're part of her estate. Amy will get them."

"What should we do, Fargo?" Harry Crew asked.

Fargo's mouth tightened as he swept the others with a long glance. He couldn't tell them so much had happened and so little had changed. "Don't default," he said grimly.

"You saying something?" someone asked.

"I've a friend, Paula. She was right about one thing. Now she's right about another. It's in the blood," he said as Amy returned with a leather traveling bag, and he helped her onto the horse. He left with her and felt the others watching him go.

He set a fast pace, anxious to get the child to Ben Hopkins, anxious to be rid of everything and anything tied to the Aversons. He realized he felt used and somehow unclean, as though he'd helped do the wrong things for the wrong people right from the start. He reached the bank and deposited Amy with Ben Hopkins as he told the banker all that had happened. "I'll see to everything," the man said. "Burials, estate matters, Amy, everything." He paused where Amy sat on the bench outside the bank, swinging her legs idly. Anyone passing would see a typical, nonchalant, terribly pretty ten-year-old. There are all kinds of masks, he murmured to himself as he swung onto his horse and rode away.

He set a fast pace to the only thing he'd really done right. She was standing by a fence post when he reined to a halt, liquid brown eyes full of promise. He noted the small clothes bag beside her. "I thought we'd go away somewhere," Loretta said.

"Best damn thought I've heard in a long time," Fargo said and swung her into the saddle with him. He'd find a spot for them to forget the world. But it wouldn't be in Blood Canyon.

LOOKING FORWARD!
The following is the opening
section from the next novel in the exciting
Trailsman series from Signet:

**THE TRAILSMAN #183
BAYOU BLOODBATH**

*1861, Louisiana bayou country...
where quicksand, gators, and cottonmouths
were the least of a man's worries...*

The scream knifed through the muggy air like cold steel through human flesh.

It caused birds to take wing in startled flight. It spooked deer into bounding off into the brush. Even several alligators raised their heads to listen.

They were not the only ones.

A big man clad in buckskins reined up his pinto stallion and cocked his head to pinpoint the direction the scream came from. Piercing lake-blue eyes surveyed the bayou country that stretched before him. The winding wetlands, broken by dense tangles of vegetation, were home to many predators, both wild beasts and the two-legged kind. As the scream just proved, it did not do for anyone to let down their guard when traveling through southern Louisiana.

Excerpt from BAYOU BLOODBATH

Skye Fargo loosened his Colt in its holster and kneed the Ovaro forward. The woman who voiced that cry had to be in dire trouble. Since he had never been one to turn his back on a lady in distress, he decided to find out what was going on and to help her if she needed it.

The Trailsman's instincts did not let him down. Sticking to solid ground, he wound deeper into the lush growth until he heard muffled voices ahead. Slowing, he passed through a stand of weeping willows and halted shy of a grassy area.

Four men surrounded a lovely brunette wearing a tight homespun dress. She was flat on her back, her green eyes wide with fear. Her fright seemed to strike them as humorous. One poked her with a boot, then laughed when she cringed. Another grabbed at her hair, but she jerked her head away.

"Is that any way to treat your old friend Lacombe? After all the times I've been to your house, *chere*?"

The man named Lacombe was tall and lanky. He wore dark pants, a dark shirt, and a black coat that hung clear down to his ankles. A shock of brown hair crowned his hawkish features. Bending, he hooked a finger under the woman's chin and blew a kiss at her.

"You do remember how friendly I tried to be, don't you, *mon petit*?"

Another man in shabby clothes slipped a grimy hand into a pocket and pulled out a length of rope. "What are we waitin' for, Henri? Let's get this over with. I ain't got all year." He reached for the woman's arm, but she cowered back. "Make it easy on yourself, wench, or we'll have to get rough."

Skye Fargo had seen enough. He spurred the pinto into

Excerpt from BAYOU BLOODBATH

the open, his right hand resting on the butt of his pistol. "I'm new to these parts, gents, but I know this isn't how most men in Louisiana treat pretty females. I'd back off if I were you."

The man with the rope stiffened. "Who the hell is he? What's he doing here?"

A third ruffian in a floppy hat took a few steps toward the stallion. He had a face that looked as if it had been sat on by a bear, and a Remington revolver tucked under his wide brown leather belt. "You picked the wrong place to be at the wrong time, mister. Turn that nag around and get going or you'll regret it."

Fargo never had taken kindly to being threatened. Kneeing the pinto so it turned broadside to the scruffy gunman, he said, "It must be hard going through life as dumb as an ox. Makes a man wonder how you've lived as long as you have." He watched the ruffian's dark eyes. They would give him the telltale clue.

The gunman glanced at Henri Lacombe, who nodded. Smirking, the man then planted his feet wide, saying, "I'm not half as dumb as you, mister. At least I know better than to butt into things that are none of my affair." His hand lowered to within an inch of the Remington. "Any last words, busybody?"

"A few," Fargo said.

"Let's hear them."

Fargo had not taken his eyes off the gunman's. "Did you have any idea when you got up this morning that this was the last day of your life?" He saw anger flush the man scarlet, saw the slight tightening of the eyes that told him what the gunman was going to do.

They drew. The gunman must have fancied himself

Excerpt from BAYOU BLOODBATH

fast, but he had deluded himself. Fargo's Colt was out and leveled before the other man's pistol cleared the leather. He had the hammer curled back before the barrel straightened, and squeezed the trigger the instant it did.

The slug caught the gunman in the sternum, punching him backward. Tottering wildly, he crashed to earth at the feet of Henri Lacombe. No one else so much as twitched. Lacombe cracked a sly smile, then whistled in appreciation. "I thought I'd seen some fine shootin' in my time, *monsieur*. But you top everything."

Fargo cocked the Colt and pointed it at Lacombe. "I can do it again if you liked it so much. I can do it three more times, in fact."

The cutthroats with Lacombe exchanged worried looks.

Henri Lacombe chuckled. "*Homme d'esprit*, eh? No, that won't be necessary. We'll be going now. You've made your point." Raising his hands in mock surrender, he started to back off.

"You're putting the cart before the horse," Fargo said grimly. "I'm not done yet."

"How so?"

"Take off your boots and your pants."

Lacombe visibly tensed. His companions looked more worried, one nervously licking his lips. "You can't be serious, *monsieur*. You'd make us walk all the way back half undressed? Through the *swamps*?"

Fargo shrugged. "Maybe it will teach you some manners. I wouldn't want to hear that you make a habit of pushing young women around. I'd have to look you up if I did. You wouldn't want that."

Unlike the gunman, Lacombe was too shrewd to let his

Excerpt from BAYOU BLOODBATH

feathers be ruffled. He smiled again, a devious twinkle in his gaze. "You and me, *homme*, we are a lot alike, I think."

"Shuck those boots and pants."

The other two hesitated, obeying only when Lacombe laughed and told them to comply. Fargo let them keep their underwear on, such as it was. The burliest of the cutthroats wore a pair that had not been washed in ten years, if that. The other had so many holes in his that there was not enough wool left to feed a starved moth. They glared at him the whole time they were undressing.

Henri Lacombe was different. He hummed to himself, neatly folded his pants, and set his shoes side by side. Straightening, he winked at the brunette. "How about this sight, *chere*? Three half-naked men. What would your mother say?"

"Pick a direction and walk," Fargo commanded. Suddenly, the burly character clenched his fists and made as if to rush him. Feeling charitable, Fargo snapped a shot into the ground close to the man's dirty toes. "I'd think twice before I'd do that again," he advised.

Lacombe slapped his companion's shoulder. "Enough, Wilson! Are you tryin' to get us killed? We go while we can. There are always other days." Backing off, he gave a little wave. "I can't say it's been all that pleasant, *monsieur*, but I can say it has been educational. When next we meet, I will not take you lightly." Pivoting, he ambled off, whistling happily as if he did not have a care in the world. His sulking friends trailed along. Both cast longing looks at their boots and pants.

Fargo did not holster the Colt until they were out of sight. First he replaced the spent cartridge, and as he did,

Excerpt from BAYOU BLOODBATH

he noticed that the brunette had not moved. "Are you all right, ma'am?" he asked.

For some reason the simple question provoked a wellspring of tears. She sobbed once, then pushed erect and stood smoothing her wrinkled dress. "I thank you, sir, for helping me." she choked out. "It was awful kind of you." She paused to dab at her eyes. "Not that it will do any good. They'll get me in the long run. They always get the ones they're after."

"Who are they? Why do they want you?"

The brunette glanced at him, abject despair mirrored by her expression. She opened her lush mouth as if to say more, but evidently changed her mind. Pressing a hand to her forehead, she gazed in the direction Lacombe and his friends had taken, then she spun to the southwest and bounded off like a frightened antelope.

"Wait!" Fargo called out. "You have nothing to be afraid of!"

It was a waste of breath. The woman was not about to stop. Her long legs flying, she weaved among the trees and bushes with the skill of someone who had lived in bayou country all her life. He caught a flash of silken thigh before she disappeared.

Fargo sighed and shook his head. The incident had been a hell of a way to start a new day. Clucking the pinto onward, he rode deeper into the swamp. For perhaps the hundredth time, he wondered if he wasn't making a fool of himself. He had come so far. What if it turned out to be someone's warped idea of a prank? Or a child's fantasy?

Fargo had been about to indulge in a week of wine, women, and wild times when the letter reached him.

Excerpt from BAYOU BLOODBATH

Flush with winnings from a stud poker game in Texas, he had decided to treat himself to some civilized hospitality and checked into his favorite hotel in St. Louis. The first order of business had been a hot bath in a big tub. He had been up to his neck in water and suds when the desk clerk timidly rapped on the door. "It's open," Fargo had hollered.

The mouse of a man came over holding a battered envelope. "I'm terribly sorry to bother you, sir, but the stage just came in, and this was in the mail pouch for you." He handed it over and got out of there as if embarrassed to be in the same room with someone taking a bath.

Fargo had not known what to make of the envelope. It was addressed simply, *Skye Fargo, The Trailsman*. The handwriting was the scrawl of a small child. Judging by the postmarks, the letter had been mailed from Baton Rouge to New Orleans. From there someone had sent it on to Denver. The rest were a jumble, but it appeared that the letter had followed him across the West, from Denver to Topeka, from Topeka to Forth Worth, from Fort Worth to St. Louis. It was a small miracle the thing ever caught up with him.

He had opened it, read the two sentences, and blurted, "What the hell?" The message had been short and to the point, in the same scrawl as that on the front of the envelope. "Mr. Trailsman," he read aloud. "My sister has been taken by bad men. Please come quick." The writer signed it, 'Jessica Tanner, Possum Hollow.'"

Fargo had tossed the letter onto a dresser and not given it another thought. It had been ridiculous to think that he would saddle up and head off to somewhere he had never heard of just because a girl barely old enough to write

Excerpt from BAYOU BLOODBATH

claimed her sister was in trouble. He'd bathed and dressed and gone across the street to a fancy restaurant where a sultry woman in a red dress had caught his eye.

For a while all had gone well. Fargo had introduced himself, and she had proven to be the friendly sort. After an expensive meal they had gone off to a nearby theater. That was when the damn note kept popping into his head. He'd be staring at the actors on the stage and instead see the note in his mind's eye. He'd look at the woman, and there it was again. Try as he might—and did he ever try!—he could not stop thinking about it.

Jezebel had invited Fargo to her room after the play. He'd gladly gone, hoping that the delights he was about to savor would help him forget the little girl's appeal. Yet when Jezebel stood before him in all her naked glory, he had looked at her ample bosom and seen the child's handwriting scrawled across her chest.

It had been too aggravating for words. He'd practically thrown Jezebel onto her bed and coupled with her with the ferocity of a wildcat. The scratch marks she had left had not healed for days.

At the crack of dawn Fargo had been at the stable to reclaim the Ovaro. He'd booked passage for himself and the horse on a steamboat heading south down the mighty Mississippi. On arriving in Baton Rouge, he had asked around and learned that Possum Hollow was the name of a tiny town in a remote part of the bayou.

Now here he was, enduring a stifling heat and swarms of mosquitoes, always on the lookout for poisonous snakes and giant gators, wishing he was anywhere but where he was, and all because a child had pleaded for his aid. Sometimes he amazed himself.

Excerpt from BAYOU BLOODBATH

It was interesting that the brunette had gone in the same direction he was headed. It might mean that Possum Hollow was not far ahead. No one in Baton Rouge had been able to tell him exactly how many miles he had to travel because no one he met in Baton Rouge had ever been to Possum Hollow. As a riverman had phrased it, "No one lives there but swamp trash, breeds, and bugs. Don't blink when you ride past, friend, or you'll miss it."

Lily pads and reeds appeared on the left. Fargo heard a bullfrog croak, another answer. The buzz of insects was a steady drone. In the grass to his right something rustled. He spied a sinuous form covered with scales, but it slithered off before he could get a good look at it. Which was just as well. The swamp crawled with cottonmouths, copperheads, and rattlesnakes. As if that were not enough, coral snakes were plentiful, too.

Having lived his whole life in the wilderness, Fargo knew all the wild creatures and their habits. He had learned to live with grizzlies, wolves, mountain lions, and wolverines. He tolerated skunks, buzzards, and coyotes. But he had never, ever been very fond of snakes. The truth was, they made his skin crawl. He'd as soon shoot one as look at it, although he never did unless the reptile posed a threat.

The terrain became more marshy. Swamp closed in on both sides until the strip of dry ground was no more than thirty feet wide. Fargo was about convinced that he would have to change course when he came on a well-marked trail. The number of hoofprints and footprints told him that the trail saw regular use. For over a mile he followed it, until all of a sudden he emerged from a stand of tall trees to find a narrow valley before him.

Excerpt from BAYOU BLOODBATH

In the center was Possum Hollow. It consisted of seven shanty shacks made from uneven boards and mismatched scraps of lumber. Smoke wafted from a stovepipe jutting above the largest. A rutted excuse for a road wound among the buildings and vanished into the swampland on the far side.

The place was as quiet as a tomb. No one was about. The only living things Fargo saw were an old hog rooting around the base of a stump and a flock of chickens pecking at the dirt. He had a feeling, though, that unseen eyes were on him, that the residents of the sleepy hamlet knew he was there. How they knew, he couldn't say. Backwoods folks had their ways.

Fargo rode on, his right thumb wedged under his gunbelt close to the Colt. A flicker of movement in the darkened doorway of the first shack drew his interest. He tensed, ready to draw, then grinned when a filthy, naked toddler waddled onto the rickety porch and gawked at him as if he were an apparition. The next second a woman in a tattered dress darted outside, grabbed her offspring around the waist, and scooted back inside.

Fargo had been to some out-of-the-way spots in his time. He had visited the heart of the Everglades, gone into the Appalachian hill country. In both regions it was not uncommon to meet people who would rather keep to themselves, who were naturally suspicious of any and all strangers.

Here it was different. He had a gut feeling that there was more to the absence of the inhabitants than was apparent. The fleeting glance the mother had thrown at him had been a fearful one, almost as if she dreaded that he would do her harm.

Excerpt from BAYOU BLOODBATH

The short hairs at the nape of Fargo's neck prickled as he entered the pitiful excuse for a town. He passed a darkened window and thought he saw a vague figure staring at him. From one of the dwellings came the voice of an older child that was punctuated by a slap. He drew rein at a rickety hitching post in front of the large building. The creak of his saddle as he swung down seemed eerily loud.

Looping the reins, Fargo walked around the rail onto the plank post. On the side of the building a mule and two horses were tied. Near the door, painted in crude letters, was a sign: BIG BOB'S LIQUOR, TACK AND EMPORIUM. Fargo doubted that the man who wrote it even knew what an emporium was since the word and half the others were misspelled.

The door hung open. Fargo stepped inside, promptly stepping to the right so his back was to the wall. The interior was dim, the only source of light the sunlight streaming in through a window and the doorway. Two tables and chairs filled the middle of the floor. On one side was a counter, on the other a stove on which a pot of coffee perked. Shelves lined all the walls, most crammed with dusty merchandise.

Guessing who was known as Big Bob was not hard. A man the size of a mountain lounged against the counter. A dirty apron hung around his ample waist. Fleshy jowls and flabby arms quivered when he moved, as if he were made of pudding and not flesh and blood. Regarding Fargo coldly, he said, "Howdy, stranger. We don't get many pilgrims passing through these parts."

Fargo was studying the other two. They were brothers, one a few years older than the other, but so alike in their scarecrow frames, unkempt black hair, and faded home-

Excerpt from BAYOU BLOODBATH

spun clothes that there was no mistaking the resemblance. The older one had a butcher knife in a hip sheath and a Sharps rifle held in the crook of an elbow. His brother was partial to a Bowie knife and a pistol worn butt forward on the left hip. They met his stare, and theirs was not friendly.

"What will it be?" Big Bob asked. "I've got whiskey and ale." He moved behind the counter. "If you think you can handle it, I've also got some local brew that would grow hair on a bald man."

The brothers snickered at Bob's little joke. Fargo crossed to the counter, positioning himself so that he could keep one eye on the door and the other on Bob and his customers. Through the window he could see the Ovaro. "A glass of whiskey will wash down the dust," he said.

"Coming right up." Big Bob had to stoop to reach under the counter. Selecting a glass, he wiped it with his apron, filled it halfway, and brought the glass over. "That'll be a dollar."

"For one drink?" Fargo said.

Big Bob jabbed a thick thumb at the assorted bottles lining a shelf. "Do you think I get this stuff brought in from Baton Rouge for free? They charge me extra if they bring it themselves, so twice a year I have to go up there with a pack horse and tote back a couple of cases."

Fargo swallowed, savoring the burning sensation that scorched his throat and stomach. At least the whiskey was not watered down. Fishing in his pocket, he removed two gold quarter eagles and slapped them on the wood.

Bob's bushy eyebrows puckered. "You must want a whole bottle."

Excerpt from BAYOU BLOODBATH

"I want information," Fargo set him straight. "You can keep the change if you can help me out." He took another sip. "I need directions to the Tanner place."

Something happened. Fargo detected a change in the three men, a barely noticeable tensing, and in Bob's case a twitching of those heavy jowls. The brothers whispered, then stared at him more coldy than ever. "I know the Tanners live around here. You must know them."

"Can't say as I do," Big Bob said. He turned. "How about you two boys? You've lived in these parts all your lives. Ever heard tell of a family by that name?"

The older brother answered. "Can't rightly say as we have. What's your business with them, anyway, mister?"

"It's *my* business," Fargo stressed. Polishing off his drink, he picked up the eagles and slapped a dollar on the counter in their place. "No information, no tip."

Big Bob stared wistfully at the pocket the gold eagles had gone into. "We didn't mean to rile you none, stranger. These boys are the Genritt brothers, Buck and Morco. If Buck says he's never heard of them, then someone must have sent you on a wild-goose chase."

It was so obvious that they were lying that Fargo was tempted to force them to tell the truth. But the other locals might not take too kindly to having some of their own pistol whipped. Walking outdoors, he surveyed Possum Hollow. The chickens were gone, leaving the street all to the hog. It ambled toward him, grunting noisily, maybe hoping for a handout.

Unhitching the Ovaro, Fargo led it to the next building. The door was closed, so he knocked. Footsteps scraped within, and there were muted voices. No one, though, re-

Excerpt from BAYOU BLOODBATH

sponded to his knock. He tried again with the same result. Whoever was inside wanted nothing to do with him.

Five shacks were left. Fargo walked to the next. Flowers had been planted under a window covered by burlap. Through a crack an eyeball peeked out at him. He pretended not to see it and halted in front of a door someone had left cracked open. "Hello?" he said. "I'd like a word with you, if you don't mind."

The same pattern repeated itself. Feet pattered. Muttering broke out. Fargo rapped his knuckles on the jamb. "I don't mean any harm. I'd just like some information. Please. Open the door."

His request was granted, but not in the manner Fargo expected. The door was abruptly flung wide, and he found himself looking down the barrel of a cocked rifle.

① SIGNET (0451)

BLAZING NEW TRAILS WITH THE ACTION-PACKED TRAILSMAN SERIES BY JON SHARPE

- [ ] THE TRAILSMAN #119: RENEGADE RIFLES (170938—$3.50)
- [ ] THE TRAILSMAN #124: COLORADO QUARRY (172132—$3.50)
- [ ] THE TRAILSMAN #125: BLOOD PRAIRIE (172388—$3.50)
- [ ] THE TRAILSMAN #134: COUGAR DAWN (175034—$3.50)
- [ ] THE TRAILSMAN #135: MONTANA MAYHEM (175271—$3.50)
- [ ] THE TRAILSMAN #136: TEXAS TRIGGERS (175654—$3.50)
- [ ] THE TRAILSMAN #137: MOON LAKE MASSACRE (175948—$3.50)
- [ ] THE TRAILSMAN #138: SILVER FURY (176154—$3.50)
- [ ] THE TRAILSMAN #140: THE KILLING CORRIDOR (177517—$3.50)
- [ ] THE TRAILSMAN #141: TOMAHAWK JUSTICE (177525—$3.50)
- [ ] THE TRAILSMAN #142: GOLDEN BULLETS (177533—$3.50)
- [ ] THE TRAILSMAN #143: DEATHBLOW TRAIL (177541—$3.50)
- [ ] THE TRAILSMAN #144: ABILENE AMBUSH (177568—$3.50)
- [ ] THE TRAILSMAN #146: NEBRASKA NIGHTMARE (178769—$3.50)
- [ ] THE TRAILSMAN #148: CALIFORNIA QUARRY (178831—$3.50)
- [ ] THE TRAILSMAN #149: SPRINGFIELD SHARPSHOOTERS (178858—$3.50)
- [ ] THE TRAILSMAN #150: SAVAGE GUNS (178866—$3.50)
- [ ] THE TRAILSMAN #151: CROW HEART'S REVENGE (178874—$3.50)
- [ ] THE TRAILSMAN #152: PRAIRIE FIRE (178882—$3.99)
- [ ] THE TRAILSMAN #153: SAGUARRO SHOWDOWN (178890—$3.99)
- [ ] THE TRAILSMAN #154: AMBUSH AT SKULL PASS (178904—$3.99)
- [ ] THE TRAILSMAN #155: OKLAHOMA ORDEAL (178912—#3.99)
- [ ] THE TRAILSMAN #156: SAWDUST TRAIL (181603—#3.99)
- [ ] THE TRAILSMAN #157: GHOST RANCH MASSACRE (181611—$3.99)
- [ ] THE TRAILSMAN #158: TEXAS TERROR (182154—#3.99)
- [ ] THE TRAILSMAN #159: NORTH COUNTRY GUNS (182162—$3.99)
- [ ] THE TRAILSMAN #160: TORNADO TRAIL (182170—$3.99)

Prices slightly higher in Canada.

Buy them at your local bookstore or use this convenient coupon for ordering.

PENGUIN USA
P.O. Box 999 — Dept. #17109
Bergenfield, New Jersey 07621

Please send me the books I have checked above.
I am enclosing $_____ (please add $2.00 to cover postage and handling). Send check or money order (no cash or C.O.D.'s) or charge by Mastercard or VISA (with a $15.00 minimum). Prices and numbers are subject to change without notice.

Card #_____ Exp. Date _____
Signature_____
Name_____
Address_____
City _____ State _____ Zip Code _____

For faster service when ordering by credit card call **1-800-253-6476**

Allow a minimum of 4-6 weeks for delivery. This offer is subject to change without notice.

SIGNET

LEGENDS OF THE WEST

☐ **SCARLET PLUME by Frederick Manfred.** Amid the bloody 1862 Sioux uprising, a passion that crosses all boundaries is ignited. Judith Raveling is a white woman captured by the Sioux Indians. Scarlet Plume, nephew of the chief who has taken Judith for a wife, is determined to save her. But surrounded by unrelenting brutal fighting and vile atrocities, can they find a haven for a love neither Indian nor white woman would sanction? (184238—$4.50)

☐ **RIDERS OF JUDGMENT by Frederick Manfred.** Full of the authentic sounds and colors of the bloody Johnson County range wars of the 1890s, this tale of Cain Hammett and his devotion to his family and his land, captures the heroism of a long-vanished era. When the cattle barons invade Cain's territory, this man of peace must turn to his guns and avenge all that has been taken from him. "A thriller all the way."—*New York Times* (184254—$4.99)

☐ **WHITE APACHE by Frank Burleson.** Once his name was Nathanial Barrington, one of the finest officers in the United States Army. Now his visions guide him and his new tribe on daring raids against his former countrymen. Amid the smoke of battle and in desire's fiercest blaze, he must choose between the two proud peoples who fight for his loyalty and the two impassioned women who vie for his soul. (187296—$5.99)

☐ **WHISPERS OF THE MOUTAIN by Tom Hron.** White men had come to Denali, the great sacred mountain looming over the Indians' ancestral land in Alaska, searching for gold that legend said lay hidden on its heights. A shaman died at the hands of a greed-mad murderer—his wife fell captive to the same human monster. Now in the deadly depth of winter, a new hunt began on the treacherous slopes of Denali—not for gold but for the most dangerous game of all. (187946—$5.99)

☐ **WHISPERS OF THE RIVER by Tom Hron.** Passion and courage, greed and daring—a stirring saga of the Alaskan gold rush. With this rush of brawling, lusting, striving humanity, walked Eli Bonnet, a legendary lawman who dealt out justice with his gun . . . and Hannah Twigg, a woman who dared death for love and everything for freedom. (187806—$5.99)

*Prices slightly higher in Canada

Buy them at your local bookstore or use this convenient coupon for ordering.

PENGUIN USA
P.O. Box 999 — Dept. #17109
Bergenfield, New Jersey 07621

Please send me the books I have checked above.
I am enclosing $_____ (please add $2.00 to cover postage and handling). Send check or money order (no cash or C.O.D.'s) or charge by Mastercard or VISA (with a $15.00 minimum). Prices and numbers are subject to change without notice.

Card #_____ Exp. Date _____
Signature_____
Name_____
Address_____
City _____ State _____ Zip Code _____

For faster service when ordering by credit card call **1-800-253-6476**

Allow a minimum of 4-6 weeks for delivery. This offer is subject to change without notice.